C000021507

"*Secret Legacy kept me spellbound from page one to the very last word! The tension and relationships are beautifully written and will keep readers coming back for more. I got chills up my spine more than once. I can't wait to see what happens next.*"

— JJ KING, USAT BESTSELLING AUTHOR

"*A whimsical tale that will transport you from the first page.*"

— CARLYLE LABUSCHAGNE, USAT
BESTSELLING AUTHOR

"This book is packed full of awesomeness! Supernatural academy? Check. A girl who feels like she doesn't belong? Check. Sexy, mysterious boy? Check. And alllll the secrets, twists, and turns to keep you flipping pages. You don't want to miss this one!"

— LIZA STREET, USAT BESTSELLING
AUTHOR

Original Copyright © 2020 Carissa Andrews

Published in 2020 by Carissa Andrews

Cover Design © Carissa Andrews

All rights reserved.

ISBN-13: 978-1-953304-02-5

SOUL LEGACY

Book 2 of the Windhaven Witches

CARISSA ANDREWS

CHAPTER 1
LOOSE ENDS

After everything we've been through, why this?

"You can't be serious, Wade. Everything is almost done here at Mistwood Point and you'll be free to move to Windhaven. We have more than enough room at my dad's house. Why on earth would you want to get an apartment?" I say, combing my fingers through my hair.

Wade sets down the cardboard box, letting it teeter precariously on top of a small stack of others just like it. "I know you don't get it, and to be honest, it's hard to explain. I guess after everything that's gone on, I just don't think I'm comfortable with that. It's not you, not at all. This whole thing with my grandpa, going through all of his belongings and life history—it hit me harder than I expected, and I just need some space alone to think."

My heart skips a beat, practically plummeting into my stomach.

Alone.

Not a good sign.

Taking a deep breath, I pinch the bridge of my nose. This is also about the conversation with the man at the cemetery last fall. I know it is.

"Wade, is there anything you want to tell me? Anything that's been on your mind since...I don't know, your grandpa's funeral?" I ask, once again trying to open the door that will allow him to be honest with me.

His silver eyes widen, and he blinks back surprise. Holding very still for a moment, his gaze turns downward and his jaw clenches. "I—not really. I mean, I know I've been a bit off. It's just...losing everyone who's related to you, it kind of cuts a hole, you know? I need to make sure I'm in a good place for us."

I nod, trying to ignore the sinking feeling. "I get that."

There's a ring of truth to his words, but I can sense there's so much more in the undercurrents of his thoughts. Why won't he open up to me?

I narrow my gaze, watching his movements.

He fidgets with the lid of the box, refusing to look back up at me. "Besides, after taking care of everything here, the last thing I want to do is bring you down before the new semester starts. Getting some independence again will help me get grounded, literally."

"I understand wanting space and independence, and I'm trying to be supportive of whatever you need. It's just —there's plenty of space at the manor. Take a whole wing, if you want. I don't mind," I say, standing up and walking over to him. I place my hand on his upper arm, hoping he'll hold me close.

He twists around, wrapping his arms around me. "It's not that simple, Autumn. I wish I could explain it in a way that makes sense for you, but it doesn't even fully make sense to me. You'll have to just trust me. This is for the best."

"It doesn't feel like it..." I whisper, blinking back tears.

"Hey, don't be sad. This isn't goodbye. Not at all. I'm moving closer, remember?" he says, tipping my chin up to look at him.

I nod. "I know."

His lips curve upward as he traces my eyebrow with his pointer finger. "This will work out really well, you'll see."

He places his chin on the top of my head and we stand in the middle of his grandpa's living room, both of us refusing to make a move. There are so many unanswered questions and feelings of upheaval.

I know I'm going to have to ask him outright about what I saw at the graveyard, but I need to build up the courage first. It's been weeks, and neither one of us have brought it up. I had hoped by now he would have opened up to me on his own time. Instead, I've had to go into research mode, trying to figure out who the man was. Of course, with absolutely no luck whatsoever.

"Wade, I need to ask you something..." I begin.

His gaze lifts to mine, but the moment is broken by a knock on the door. He holds up a finger. "Hold that thought, okay?"

I exhale, letting my shoulders relax.

Wade shoots me an apologetic look and walks to the front door.

"Can I help you?" he asks, standing in the doorway with one hand resting on the frame.

I crane my head, trying to get a better view. A short man with a dark comb-over and navy-blue suit stands in the doorway. It's not the man from the graveyard, but his appearance screams "official business."

"Mr. Hoffman, good. I was hoping you'd be here. I've been trying to get in touch, but you're a difficult man to get ahold of," the man says, pulling his briefcase forward and clutching it to his chest. "We have a date for the official reading of the will."

Wade nods, sweeping his right arm out to allow the man inside.

The man tips his head and steps into the entry, then walks to the living room. When he sees me, he smiles and says, "Ma'am."

"Please, it's Autumn," I say, holding my hand out.

He takes my hand, giving it a good shake. "David Moore. Mr. Hoffman's estate attorney."

"Nice to meet you," I say, shooting him a genuine smile.

Wade steps around Mr. Moore and cleans off the small coffee table in the middle of the room.

Taking the hint, the lawyer drops his briefcase and clicks it open. Inside is a large manilla envelope, which he pulls out, and then snaps the case shut.

"Here are the details. The closing for the house is set for the first Friday of January, and we will go over the reading of the will two weeks from then. All of the location details are in the envelope, as well as the information we've received from your grandfather and you. I'd like for you to review it to make sure there's nothing we're missing," he says, handing Wade the packet.

Wade clears his throat, swallowing hard. He takes the envelope and drops his arm to his side without even looking at it.

"Okay," he mumbles.

Mr. Moore's lips press tightly, and he attempts a smile. "I truly am sorry for your loss, Wade. Your grandfather was a good man. I thoroughly enjoyed our talks through the years. He was very fond of you."

"Yeah," Wade says, biting on the inside of his cheek.

The awkward silence fills the space between them, and I step forward. "Is there anything else he needs to take care of? Or is that all?"

Mr. Moore takes a step back and shakes his head. "No, that's all for today. I just needed to make sure in person that Mr. Hoffman was aware of these final details. Thank you both for allowing me to take the time. Have a nice night." He pats Wade on the shoulder and turns back the way they came in. Wade doesn't move a muscle. Instead, his forehead is scrunched in thought.

"Here, I'll show you out," I say, stepping around them both and leading the way.

I open the door and smile as Mr. Moore steps out onto the front steps. He nods but continues on his way. When he's gotten into his black Lexus, I close the door and turn back to Wade.

"Everything okay?" I say, entering the living room. Wade hasn't moved from where I left him.

He flings the packet onto the coffee table and nods.

"You knew this was coming, right? I mean, isn't this what you wanted?" I ask. "To finally have it all come to a close?"

"Yeah, it is. It's just...strange, you know?" he says, trying to smooth out the pained expression that's taken over his features.

I nod. "I can imagine. But this is good. It means the

end is near and you'll be able to move on with your own journey. You've done a lot these past few weeks. I've been impressed by how you've known exactly what to do. I mean, if it were me, I'd still be fumbling."

"I had to learn quickly, I guess. Grandpa was pretty specific on what he wanted. It made it easier," he says.

"So...what's on your mind, then?" I say, walking around so I can be in his direct line of sight.

His pupils dilate and he attempts a smile. "I'm just a little worried to find out how it all is going to look, you know?"

"Why?"

"Grandpa had a lot of additional help these past few months and any inheritance I get is supposed to cover my tuition at Windhaven Academy. But I know end-of-life help doesn't come cheap and the county will want to recoup the cost. So..."

"You're worried you won't be able to swing it?" I say, finishing his thought.

He nods, screwing up his lips.

"That, I totally get. There's no way I would have been able to pay for Windhaven Academy, either. But surely with the sale of the house and everything, the funds will cover most of it, right?"

Wade shrugs. "Maybe? I mean, I sure hope so. If not, I have no idea what I'm gonna do."

Walking over to him, I wrap my arms around his waist. "If it comes to that, we'll figure it out."

He chuckles softly. "You don't owe me anything, Dru. You need to worry about you. This semester is going to be amazing for you. Especially now that you know more about your powers."

My lips curve upward at his pet name for me. Maybe he's coming back around?

"It's not about owing anything. It's about taking care of each other. That's what we do, right?" I say, giving him a squeeze. "Besides, it's going to be incredible having you at the academy. I'll be able to show you all of the cool places and I'm excited to see what kind of abilities you might possess. It's almost like our roles have reversed."

Wade places his hands on my upper arms, pulling back from me. "I wouldn't get your hopes up. There's a good chance my gifts won't manifest at all."

I snicker. "What are you talking about?"

Shaking his head, he takes a step back. "Sometimes they skip generations."

"Well, wouldn't you want to know for sure before going to Windhaven Academy? I mean, why work on developing powers you don't know if you even have?"

"You tell me? What was the allure?" he says, raising his eyebrows.

I take a step back and nod. "Point taken."

"Look, my family's gifts often lie dormant until triggered. I don't know when, or if, they will come. But what I do know is that I need to learn more about how to manage them if they're triggered. I can't do that anywhere else. It's not like I have any family members left to ask," he says, frowning.

"Good point," I whisper, considering his words. "Wade...this might not be the best time to ask, but I need to know something. It's been on my mind for a while."

He runs a hand through his hair and takes a seat on the arm of the sofa. "What is it?"

I swallow hard, wringing my hands in front of my body

as I search for the right words. "Look, I probably should have brought this up sooner, it's just..."

"Spit it out, woman. The suspense is killing me," he says, concern painting his tone.

"The day we buried your grandpa, I saw you talking with someone," I say, beginning to pace.

"Right, the guy looking for the caretaker?" Wade says, nodding.

I stop pacing and turn to him. Pinching my face tight, I say, "Mmmm... It kinda seemed like you two knew each other."

His eyes narrow and he tilts his head. "Autumn, I don't know what to tell you."

I double-take, stumbling backward. "I swear I heard him arguing with you."

Wade stands up, his eyebrows tugging in, but he doesn't respond.

"I've seen him before," I say. "He spoke to me when I was at Cat's accident."

"How do you know it was the same guy? I mean, there are lots of—"

"He billowed in from some sort of portal and...took the souls from the Vodník's jar. He's not just a person, he's something else, but I don't know what. When he left after the conversation with you, he vanished the same way. I know it was the same guy," I say, jutting out my chin.

"Okay? People get around, especially travelers, if that's what he was. So, what did he say to you?" Wade asks, his face still stoic.

"He told me he'd be back. And that I can only meddle for so long..."

For the first time, his face flickers. "Well, that seems ominous. Did he tell you why? Or who he was?"

"No, but he knew I was a necromancer before I did. I mean, before I ever used my powers to save Cat," I say. I watch his mannerisms closely, but Wade remains an unreadable statue. My shoulders drop and my eyebrows tug in.

Why is he lying to me? What on earth is he hiding?

CHAPTER 2
WITCHING STICK, TAKE 2

A snow-covered Windhaven Academy looms in front of us and despite its serene appearance, anxiety can't help but make a home in my mind.

The last time we tried to attend a Witching Stick orientation day, the school was in total chaos. Intellectually, I know this is a new day—*a new semester*. But a part of me is still on edge, like something could go sideways at any moment. If for no other reason than the weird vibe growing between Wade and me.

I'd thought we'd be growing closer by the time he moved here. Not the other way around.

"You ready to head inside?" Wade asks, putting his Impala in park.

I turn to him and chuckle softly. "Shouldn't I be asking you that?"

"It's just a school, right?" He shrugs, then quirks an eyebrow. "Besides, it's not like I haven't been here before."

"Yes, but this is literally as far as you got last time," I

say, shooting him a knowing look. "Well, okay, so you made it inside the doorway."

"True, true," he nods. "On the upside, it still stands. No hellmouth or anything. And it *is* a pretty nice door." His grin beams back at me and makes my heart flutter.

I shake my head, trying to chase away this anxiety and let his lighter mood take root. Yet it still sits there like a rock in the pit of my stomach. I want to reach out to him, touch his face, and tell him how I'm feeling, but...

"Come on," I finally say, kicking open my door.

Wade follows after me, circling around the front of his car and reaching out to take my hand. I slide my palm against his and we walk through the sea of cars toward the massive structure. Our feet crunch against the snow glittering the ground, and I tug my coat in tighter.

"So, anything I should know? Best people to go to for help, or places to avoid when I don't want to study?" Wade asks, nudging me in the shoulder.

"Well, for sure, the person to talk to is Ms. Cain for almost everything. She's a strange duck, for sure, but she'll know how to point you in the right direction. I swear, she's a walking encyclopedia."

"Good to know. Can you point her out when we get inside?" he says, his breath billowing out in clouds in the chill morning air. Even the tip of his nose has begun to turn pink.

"You can't miss her. She's the main admin. We have to go to her to first," I say, reaching for the handle of the massive door.

"Cool. Makes things easy," Wade says, grabbing hold of the door as it opens and shooing me through. He gives me a sideways glance and shakes his head. "That's my job, woman."

My lips curve upward and I step to the side, allowing people to go around us. "I know how to open a door, Angel."

"I'm sure you do. That's not the point," Wade says, giving me a knowing look.

"Hey there, guys," a familiar voice rings out.

I look up, surprised to see Cat bounding down the hallway and heading toward us. Her black hair is twisted into a bun on the top of her head and she's dressed up like one of the head mistresses you'd see in Harry Potter or something. Regardless of all of that, she looks good. Like she's finally gotten the rest she desperately needed so her body could heal after the car accident and everything that followed.

Trailing behind her is Colton, dressed in a grey suit and a tie that doesn't exactly look uniform. Despite his obvious attempt at also dressing up, he remains ever the same when his gaze locks on the floor as he shuffles toward us.

When Cat reaches me, she wraps her arms around my neck and holds on tight. My eyes widen as I look at Wade, whose eyebrows rise into his hairline. I wrap my arms around her, returning her embrace.

"Cat, why are you here? You don't need orientation. Besides, shouldn't you still be in bed?" I ask, pulling back. "I thought the doctors were giving you a couple of weeks more before your system was back to normal?"

"I couldn't spend another day in that room. I was about to climb the walls. Besides, Ms. Cain asked Colton and me to help with new student tours, so...here we are."

She beams, turning back to Colton. "What are you doing back there? Yeesh, you're so awkward."

Colton juts out his chin, but his lips slide into a sideways grin.

"Yeah, uh, sorry guys. Good to see you both," he says, glancing between me and Wade before his gaze drops back to the floor.

My insides clench, and I bite my lip. I haven't spoken to Colton since the day we resurrected Cat—and the day he kissed me. It's just been too weird.

Clearing my throat, I step forward, sweeping my hand out to the side. "Guys, you remember my boyfriend, Wade, right?"

Cat grins broadly. "Yep, sure do. We didn't get much time to chat, but I feel like I know everything about you. Autumn is absolutely enamored."

Shooting her a sideways glance, I mutter under my breath, "Cat."

She takes a step backward, shaking her head. "I, uh... I meant to say, I'm totally looking forward to getting to know you, Wade." A big, cheesy grin erupts on her face and she raises her eyebrows. Then she shifts her gaze back to me like whatever she just said totally made up for the humiliation I feel coming my way.

I run my hand over my face.

Wade chuckles, turning from me to Cat. "The feeling is mutual. Autumn's told me a lot about you both. I'm looking forward to being around more." His eyes float to Colton, who glances up just in time to catch Wade's discerning gaze. The tension between the two of them settles between us like a heavy fog.

Inhaling sharply, I take Wade's hand and say, "Well, on

that note, we better get moving. We have to go see Ms. Cain and get Wade to his orientation session. See you guys around?"

"Okay, catch ya around. If you end up in the Elemental Magic wing, stop by and say hi. It's where we'll be," Cat says, spinning around on her heel as I drag Wade past them and down the hall.

"Sounds good. We'll come find you," I say, waving.

Cat waves back, but Colton grabs hold of her arm, dragging her down the hallway in the opposite direction. He leans closer, whispering something in her ear, and she glances back at us with a confused look.

Shaking it off, we walk through the open door to the admissions office and get in line. There are a lot more people here this semester, and a lot less panic going on in the halls. It's a nice change. My spirits lift a little bit.

Maybe this semester will be different? Maybe I'll finally get into a groove, learn more about my powers, and get to have my boyfriend by my side. Maybe...all of my worries are completely unfounded.

Leaning in to Wade, I whisper, "I promise you, I have only said good things to Cat."

A soft chuckle escapes his lips. "I'm not worried about that." He shifts to his other foot and itches his eyebrow. "I am, however, still concerned about her brother."

I swallow hard. "Why?"

"I read people pretty well, and there's something going on with him," he says.

"Well, his twin sister recently died and came back," I say under my breath. "I'm sure that messes with a person."

Wade shakes his head. "No, that's not it. I mean, maybe it's some of it—but he's not weird with her. He's weird around *you*. Or maybe just me. Either way, it tells me he's still got a thing for you. He hasn't tried anything, has he?"

My eyes widen and my pulse skyrockets. This is hardly the time or place to explain everything that happened. "I uh, what do you—"

"Next," Ms. Cain calls out in her bored drawl.

"I think she means us," Wade says, leaning in and tilting his head toward the desk.

Surprised, I twist around him to have a look. Ms. Cain's eyes blink slowly behind her thick-rimmed glasses, and she waves us forward.

"Oh, yeah. Hi. Hello, Ms. Cain. How have you been?" I sputter, trying to reign in my racing pulse.

She quirks a mousy-brown eyebrow over the top rim of her bold, black glasses.

I clear my throat. "This is Wade. Wade Hoffman. He's a new student and taking part in the festivities today."

"Festivities? Haven't quite heard it put that way before. Are you trying to be humorous, Ms. Blackwood?" Ms. Cain says, narrowing her gaze.

I sit there for a moment, trying to decide if she's messing with me, or if she's serious. It's so hard to tell.

"Don't get your knickers in a twist. Breathe—you'll live longer," she finally says, passing a packet of information over the granite countertop. "Mr. Hoffman, if I could get your ID and signature on the top form, I'd greatly appreciate it. It allows us to bill the card on file for tuition."

Wade's complexion pales and he licks his lower lip. "Uh, sure. Absolutely." He reaches into his back pocket, pulling out his wallet and sliding his driver's license across to her.

"Thank you," she says in her slow lilt, taking the ID and running it through a tiny scanner on the side of her desk. "Should all hell *not* break loose, you'll be taking pictures today for your student ID. Just in case, and until it's ready, this will help me put a face to your name. Plus, if we need to hunt you down, it has your address on it."

Wade glances my direction and tilts his head to the side. "Well, actually, this address will be changing soon. I'll be getting an apartment here in town, so..."

Ms. Cain's lips curve up into a creepy grimace of a smile. "Isn't that lovely? Well, be sure to update me when this momentous occasion occurs, would you?" She hands his ID back without even blinking.

Wade nods, accepting the card and putting it back into his wallet. "Of course. You'll be the first to know."

"I'm sure," Ms. Cain says, letting the sarcasm drip heavily from her lips.

Wade shoots a wide-eyed gaze in my direction. I shrug in return.

She is who she is. You get used to her style eventually.

He turns back to the stack of papers, flipping through the first few pages.

"You just need to sign the top one, Mr. Hoffman. The rest are just copies of what I've already emailed to you," Ms. Cain says, leaning to the side to view the line behind us.

"Right, okay," he says, swallowing hard. His lips press into a thin line and he signs his name on the line, as asked. Dropping the pen, he slides the stack of papers back to her.

"Just the top one is mine, dear," she says, handing the other back and grabbing a few more papers she had off to the side. "Here's your orientation packet. Take it to the Auditorium Hall. Everything starts in there. This day is fairly open. Once you perform the Witching Stick ceremony, you're free to roam the school and grounds in whatever fashion you deem necessary. I'm sure Ms. Blackwood here can show you around," she says, eyeing me. I smile in return and she flits her bored gaze back to Wade. "Welcome to Windhaven Academy, Mr. Hoffman. I'm sure you'll fit right in."

Wade grabs the packet of papers and holds it to his chest. "Thank you."

"My pleasure," she says without a hint of a smile. "*Next*."

Looping my arm through his, we leave the admissions office and head back out into the hallway.

Wade's silence fills the space and I turn to him. "Everything okay?"

"Yeah, yeah. For sure. It's just... I sure as hell hope my inheritance covers the tuition. This has an awful lot of zeroes," he says, making a face.

My insides twist and I can't help but sympathize with him. I'd been saving for ages to go to the U, simply because I couldn't afford to go straight into it from high school like everyone else. There was no way Mom was going to let me take out student loans, either. She'd have a conniption and go on a tirade about how student loans are put in place, so we start out our lives stuck under the thumb of Big Brother.

"I still have some money in my savings. We'll figure it out. If I have to get a job to help—" I begin.

"In no way are you helping me to pay for my tuition. Nuh-uh, that's a deal breaker," he says, shaking his head.

"Don't be ridiculous."

Waving a hand in front of him, he cuts me off. "Let's not worry about any of the real-world stuff right now. I'm in a friggin' *magical* school. Now's the time to sit back and enjoy it. I wanna see what the fuss is about, while I revel in the fact that I'm also here with the most beautiful woman in the whole world. Deal?"

I narrow my gaze.

"Deal," I say, hugging his arm closer. "Let's go see what this Witching Stick ceremony is all about."

Wade beams back at me and I lead the way to the auditorium. The seats are nearly filled already and I'm surprised at the sheer number of new students coming in, especially since this is just the second semester. It's not even the start of a new year.

When I began, I was off in my own world, focusing on so many of my own inner struggles that I never really looked around. I barely registered the sheer awesomeness of abilities coming from the others around me. Now, as someone who isn't worried about fitting in, or wondering about my powers, I guess I can breathe a bit. It's fascinating to see the questions painted across the faces of nearly everyone here. Their anxiety and excitement are palpable.

The two of us maneuver into one of the only two-seat spots left, which are off as far to the left of the stage as humanly possible.

Wade leans in close. "How do you think this thing goes? I mean, do you think the whole Sorting Hat thing was taken from this? God, I hope not."

My eyes widen and I hold back a laugh. "Wouldn't that be something? I guess, stranger things..."

"Right, we are definitely in the Upside Down," Wade nods.

"Not what I meant. I literally meant *stranger things* have happened."

His eyebrows lift upward and he laughs. "Oh, right. Habit."

"It's one of the many reasons I love you," I say, smiling.

He turns back to me, looking me over intensely. His silver irises get consumed by his pupils, but as he opens his mouth to speak, a hush falls across the crowd and his lips pinch tight. We both turn to face the stage just as a plume of purple fire dies back from the entrance of a woman in a purple pinstripe suit. Her wild, curly black and purple hair flows around her and she holds her arms out wide, palms up. A tiny smirk branches out across her face and she steps up to the microphone.

"Welcome everyone, to your Witching Stick ceremony. My name is Marva Arlo, but you probably remember me as the disembodied name on your admissions letter," she says, quirking an eyebrow and giving a knowing look as she casts her gaze out over the sea of people. "I'm Windhaven Academy's Director of Admission and I'm here to properly introduce you to the world of the supernatural and magic."

Leaning in, I whisper, "I have never seen this woman before now."

"This is probably her only gig. Then she goes back to sitting behind a desk," Wade snickers. "Makes sense as to why she had to make such a big entrance."

I cover my face, holding back a laugh. He's probably right. It's the most theatrical thing I've seen take place in the past five months.

"So let me explain to all of you hopefuls on how this

day works. The mere fact you are sitting in your seat means you have already been vetted as carrying supernatural qualities. Some of you were gifted from the day you were born; others may not even know what your gifts are quite yet. Each of us run on a supernatural spectrum, so to speak. Our job at Windhaven Academy is to help you develop at your current level and then quickly advance you into your area of magical expertise," she continues, crossing her arms behind her back and walking across the stage. "Should you be more advanced upon entry, you will be happy to know, your lessons will help you level up further. If you are a magical newbie, on the other hand..." she stops, raising her left hand, palm up to the air, "...then our lessons will start out in the basics as we test you for your innate abilities. Every classroom is warded with enchantments that detect who you are and your level of advancement. This helps to provide your instructor with the ability to teach you where you are at. At this point you might be thinking, 'This sounds great, Marva, but what does this mean?'"

The director stops pacing across the stage to look out over the audience again. Not a single one of us moves; instead, we're all thoroughly engrossed in her words. Even me.

"It means that while you might be in the same classroom with your peers, the lessons they are receiving may be vastly different from the one *you* are receiving. Does this make sense?"

Chatter breaks out over the audience and I turn to Wade. "Did I just hear what I think I heard?"

Wade's face is wide with surprise and he shrugs. "Heck if I know. What did you hear?"

"That each student is actually getting a different lesson at the same time during the same class?"

"Yup, that's what I got, too." He nods.

"Holy shit. How did I not realize this before now?" I say, my mouth gaping open.

"Er, probably because you didn't get to have this orientation?" Wade says.

Shaking my head, I turn back to the stage. I think back to all the lessons from last year and how many times I felt like I must be falling so far behind because I didn't know what powers I had—if any. And yet, the whole time, my lessons were individualized to each of us?

Mind officially blown.

"So, the way today works is not like anything you have read in books. Yes, Potter fans, I'm looking at you..." she says, her voice trailing off as she narrows her gaze. "Instead, you will be granted access to each and every room of this facility, including the outer grounds. We encourage your participation today, and quite honestly, everyday, because the more you explore, the more information we gather about your gifts. The better then, we can tailor the experience here for you. This even includes the people you are naturally drawn to. We have found over and over again, the supernatural beings we are in close proximity with have a direct correlation to the advancement of our own gifts. They offer a certain aspect that is dynamic to our own special qualities. So, pay attention to those you are drawn to. They are more than just friends; they are your energetic family. Their gifts will become a part of you in ways you cannot even begin to comprehend."

I turn to Wade, placing a hand on his knee and giving

it a squeeze. My smile falters when I see the look on his face.

"What is it?" I ask, tugging my eyebrows in.

"I really don't think you should be hanging out with Colton anymore," he says.

CHAPTER 3
WHERE DO I SIGN?

E verything's been a jumbled-up cluster since the Witching Stick.

Despite a decent afternoon wandering the campus, I haven't pressed Wade about his declaration to avoid Colton. Mostly because I don't want the awkwardness surrounding it to make things worse. And in all honesty, I don't think Wade's completely wrong. Colton does put out a strange vibe, and I don't want to give either of them the wrong impression. Plus, the further away we get from the kiss, the harder it is for me to bring it up.

I should have told Wade about it ages ago, but I keep putting it off because Wade still hasn't been honest with me about the graveyard. I know that's a flimsy excuse. Really, I should be better than that, but evidently, I'm not.

Plus, there's the whole refusal to stay at Blackwood Manor with me. And now here we are...

"Thanks for coming with me to look at apartments. I know you don't fully understand why I wanna do this, so it means a lot," Wade says, tapping the steering wheel and eyeing me from the driver's seat.

I press my lips together and attempt a sincere smile, but I'm fairly certain it looks more like a grimace. "You're right, I don't fully understand, but I know you feel this is what you need."

"It is," he says, nodding.

"Well, on the upside, if you pick this one, you won't be far from campus," I say, leaning forward and looking out through the windshield.

The dilapidated three-story building looks like something out of a horror movie, with its boarded-up windows and shutters hanging at odd angles. The snow is barely shoveled off of the sidewalk and two steps leading up to the main entrance. I can feel my features tighten.

"Oh, don't make that face. It isn't that bad," he chuckles, putting the vehicle into park.

I lean back, smoothing my expression. "Are you certain about that? I'm pretty sure I saw a dead body through one of those windows."

He twists to look at the building again. "Seriously? You saw a ghost?"

Slapping him on the arm, I say, "No, goofball. I'm totally kidding. Geez. But if you're not careful, you could slip on that sidewalk and it could claim its next victim."

"Gee, thanks," he smirks as he opens his door. "By the way, you can't do that when you really can see dead people. It's unfair. But on the upside, I could use your postmortem magic. If the dead *do* haunt this place, it's a deal breaker."

"That's the least of your worries. I'd be more concerned about the cockroaches. Or other creepy-crawlies." I shudder, making a face and following him out.

"Hey now, don't discriminate against the creepy-crawlies. They have feelings, too," he laughs, walking up to the building and pulling back the front door.

"I'm sure they do. Right before I stomp them with my foot and send them on their transcendental journey," I mutter, walking inside.

"Cold, man. So, so cold," he says, following after me.

The main entryway is more like a glorified hallway with a wall of small mailboxes plastered against the left-hand side. In its defense, it's cleaner inside than it appears from the outside.

Wade shoots me a look of surprise. "Not too bad in here."

"So far," I say, raising my eyebrows. "Still plenty of opportunity to scare me off."

"Ye have little faith, young one. Come on. The landlady said she'd meet me at apartment thirteen," he says, walking down the hallway and stopping in the middle of the T junction, trying to decide which way to go next.

I laugh under my breath and follow after him.

"Ah, yes. This way. See, not too difficult," he says, straightening his shoulders and taking the left hallway.

We walk down and turn to the sixth door on the left. The small number thirteen looks like it's been branded into the wall next to the door, which is wide open.

"Hello?" Wade calls out, entering the tiny efficiency apartment.

My eyes flit around the space, taking as much in as possible, until the landlady walks out of the bathroom drying her hands. She's barely older than the two of us, but her overall aura is that of an old soul, for sure. Her straw-berry-blond hair is piled up on the top of her head in one of those messy buns I would kill to be able to pull off and her green eyes flash with mischievous insight.

"Ah, Mr. Hoffman. Right on time," she says, setting the hand towel on the breakfast bar and thrusting her hand out.

Wade glances down and after a brief pause, shakes her hand. "Nice to meet you."

"Sorry, just wanted to make sure the bathroom was sparkling before you arrived," she says, sensing his hesitation.

"Oh, thanks. I appreciate that," he nods, shooting me a sideways glance.

The woman steps forward, her eyebrows raised, as she reaches out for me as well. "And you are…the wife?"

"Girlfriend," I say, eyeing Wade as I shake her hand. My cheeks burn at the idea of being mistaken for a married couple. "Autumn."

"Pleasure to meet you, Autumn. I'm Chelsea Hammond. I know this place doesn't look like much, but I'm working on it," she says, smiling. "There's only so much I can do at a time, though."

"It's actually quite nice," I say, clasping my hands behind my back and surveying the open floor-plan.

"Thank you. I bought the building last year and I've been working on it room by room. I know it looks like a dump outside, but I figure people aren't living outside, so it can wait. Besides, it keeps the riffraff away, if you know what I mean," she says, smirking.

"Valid point." I laugh.

Despite the somewhat small interior of the one large room and a bathroom, the apartment isn't terrible. New carpet, fresh paint, and an updated compact kitchen are also a plus. As much as I loathe to admit it, there's not much I can hate on here.

"So, will it be the two of you...?" Chelsea begins.

Wade shakes his head. "No, just me. But hopefully Autumn will visit often." He turns to me, narrowing his gaze and scrunching the side of his face.

I sigh, dropping my shoulders in defeat. "Of course."

"Did you want to take a look around? At least check out that bathroom I painstakingly scrubbed, would you?" Chelsea laughs. "It will make me feel better."

Wade nods enthusiastically. "Oh, most certainly." He glances in my direction, nodding toward the door.

"Oh, go on then. I have to see this bathroom," I laugh, shooing him with my hands.

Wade walks inside the tiny space, twirling around with his arms splayed out wide. "Look, Autumn. Not a single cockroach to be found."

I snicker. He's right. The bathroom is actually cleaner than the one I have back home, albeit much smaller.

"Yeah, yeah. I admit it, the place is better than anticipated."

Wade beams, stepping behind me and wrapping his arms around me. "So, does it mean you'll visit me here?"

"I already said I would," I say, shaking my head.

"Yeah, but that was when the landlady was staring you down," he says, placing his chin on my shoulder.

"I can still hear you," Chelsea mutters from the other room.

I burst out laughing and have to cover my mouth with my hand.

"I like *her*, too." I jab my thumb toward the doorway.

"And for $350 a month, you can't beat it. Not in this

town," Wade says, straightening his stance like he just said he was just nominated employee of the month.

My mouth pops open and I nod. "Wow, that's actually an awesome deal. How did you manage that?"

Wade shakes his head. "Beginner's luck?"

"Okay, guys...you're making me feel like I should rethink my pricing strategy here," Chelsea says, walking up to the doorway.

"Too late now. I'll take it," Wade says, holding out a hand. "Where do I sign?"

Chelsea tips her head to the kitchen counter behind her. "Lease is on the bar." She steps out of the way, allowing space for Wade and me to leave the bathroom.

Wade picks the piece of paper up by pinching both sides and holding it out in front of him like he's about to recite the Gettysburg Address.

"You can't just read it like a normal person, can you?" I say, grabbing it and putting it back on the bar so we can both look it over.

"Where's the fun in that?" he says, leaning forward and placing his elbows on the breakfast bar.

I shake my head, grinning to myself. Together, we read the document, making sure it's legit.

"Looks good to me," he shrugs.

"Same." I nod.

Without another word, he picks up the pen from the counter and signs his name. When he's done, he hands the lease to Chelsea.

"Thank you, sir. Now, all we need to take care of is the deposit and 1st month's rent. Then, all of this glory is waiting to be yours," she says, widening her arms.

Wade grins, turning to me.

"Welcome home, *lord of the manor*," I say, shaking my head.

He chuckles, pulling out his wallet and opening it. "Here's the check. It should cover everything."

"Excellent," Chelsea says, setting the lease and check on the breakfast bar. She digs into her front pocket and brandishes a key. "This is officially yours. I know the first isn't for a few more days, but the space is open. May as well move in whenever you're ready. You said the house you're in is closing, right?"

Wade nods. "Yeah, later this week."

"Well, I hope it all goes well," she says, pressing her lips tight. "I'm sure it's a little bittersweet."

"Definitely," he says, taking a deep breath.

Surprised, I take a step back, watching their exchange. It's obvious he's talked to her beyond just knowing where and when to meet.

A twinge of jealousy snakes through my insides.

Should I be concerned?

"On the upside, this will make the transition much easier," Wade continues, glancing around. "At least now I have someplace to move my stuff."

"Indeed, you do. Well, if there's nothing else, I'm going to go down to apartment twenty-two. The handyman is installing a new dishwasher and I need to breathe over his shoulder and make him nervous," Chelsea says, grinning widely and making for the door. "God, I love my job."

Wade snickers, then looks at me from the corner of his eye.

With a final glance into the apartment, Chelsea raises her hand and waves. "Have a nice rest of the day, guys. It was lovely to meet you both." Then she trots off down the hallway.

"Yup, I like her, too," Wade announces.

Despite my proclamation of liking her earlier, again, my gut clenches. I smile softly, hoping it masks the strange layer of possessiveness rearing its ugly head.

Wade walks over to the large picture window on the opposite end of the room. "Well, here it is. My first official apartment rented in my own name."

"Have you never had your own before?" I ask, surprised. "I thought before your grandpa got sick, you were out on your own."

He nods. "I was, but for the most part, I was too young to have my own lease. So I, uh, just stayed with different people." He runs his hand along the backside of his neck.

I get the distinct impression he's not overly excited about the way his earlier years were spent, so instead of pushing it, I nod.

"Feels good...but weird. You know? God, I hope I can find a job in town. My savings won't last super long. Especially considering tuition. Any ideas on where I could apply?" he asks, turning back to me.

My eyebrows rise and I step into the middle of the room. "Well, there's the library...or the Bourbon Room. Pick your poison. Food or books."

He laughs, shaking his head. "Difficult choice."

I nod. "Right? I guess there's always the hospital or nursing home, too. You know, if you want to continue your personal care assistant type work."

Wade's brows tug in. "Hmmm... Maybe? I am already certified, so there's that. I'll have to give it some thought."

"Sure."

Suddenly, the theme song to the television show *Lucifer* bursts out of Wade's pocket and he reaches for his cell phone. "Hello?" His face transforms from open to faltering in a matter of seconds. "Oh, yes. Um... I'm waiting on the funds to arrive. I should have it for you—" His eyes flick to me, then to the floor. "Yes, yes. I understand," he says, biting the side of his cheek and kicking at the carpet. "No, don't do that. I will definitely have it to you by the end of the week. Yes, thank you. I appreciate that." He pulls the phone from his ear, pressing the red button and cramming the phone back into his pocket. Everything about his energy has deflated.

"Not good, huh?" I say, walking up to him and placing a hand on his upper arm.

He screws up his face and shakes his head. "Not really. They need my first trimester's tuition by Friday or they'll have to open my spot to another student."

"Will you have the money from your grandpa by then?" I say, trying not to sound as alarmed as I feel.

He shrugs. "Probably not."

"What are you going to do?"

"I dunno. Pull a bank job?" he says flippantly.

"Wade," I groan.

"Kidding. Well, mostly kidding." He steps away, rubbing his hand over his mouth. "I don't know. I'll have to call the lawyer, I guess? Figure out if there's a way to speed up the process. If that doesn't work, then... I'll resort to plan B."

"Which is?" I ask, quirking an eyebrow.

His face turns ashen and his nostrils flare. "You probably don't wanna know."

CHAPTER 4

DESECRATED

My pulse picks up speed as I slow down Big Blue and pull into the parking lot for Wade's new apartment building. I hope to God he's received good news from the lawyer today. If not, I shudder to think of what he'll try to do in order to make things work. Especially since he seems hell-bent on not accepting help from anyone.

School starts on Monday and if he can't pay his tuition today, there's a good chance the school will give away his spot. After everything, it would be devastating for him. Especially to be this close, only to have to wait until next fall—or longer.

I park the car and take a deep breath, grounding myself for what's to come. I truly sympathize with his plight. If it hadn't been for my dad's surprise payment, I never would have been able to make it work. Just saving for the U was bad enough. The stress will eat you up alive if you let it.

It's freezing outside today. The temps have dropped below zero and even as small of a walk as it is from the parking lot to the front door, the chill can cut right through you. Making a mad dash from my vehicle to the building, I pull my coat in tight and thank the heavens for such warm gloves. The iron handle of the door is likely to remove skin at this temp. Other than the cold, when I reach the front door, I pull it back and enter without any of the previous reservations I had about the building. It's funny how much a little perspective shift makes such a big difference.

I walk down the hallway, noticing the old-fashioned sconces along the wall. The decorative embellishments suggest they were created in a different era, which makes me smile. Blackwood Manor is full of the same kind of antiquated decorations, and they add to the overall ambiance of the place. I couldn't imagine it being updated for a more modern look. It would just seem weird. This sort of decor makes me wonder if the same architects designed both buildings, or if the lighting was just the "in thing" at the time.

As I raise my hand to knock, Wade pulls back his door, ready for me.

"Hey, thought that was you," he says, swinging it open farther. His eyes sparkle, taking the edge off my nerves about his tuition.

"Really? Was I walking like an elephant or something?" I laugh, dropping my arm to my side and walking in.

He chuckles, twisting around to point behind him. "No, I saw you pull in, thanks to the extra large window currently lacking curtains."

"Ah, I see," I say, smiling. "Guess we should make a trip to the store to get some of those, huh?"

"Probably wise." He nods, closing the door with a click.

"So, go on then. What's the good news?" I say, unable to help myself.

Wade takes a step back, his eyebrows lifting into his hairline. "Well..."

"Oh no, it is good news, right?" I say, my nerves getting the better of me again.

He flinches. "Yes and no, I guess."

"Okay, you gotta give me more than that," I mutter, removing a box from one of his wooden chairs that are butted against his tiny, two-person dining room table. Setting the box on the floor, I take a seat.

He leans forward on the other chair, pressing the palms of his hands against the back of the seat. "Well, do you want the good news or the bad news first?"

"Good, *definitely good*," I sputter.

"Okay, then. Good news is," he takes a deep breath through his nostrils, "I can pay tuition for this semester."

"Yay," I say, clasping my hands together as relief floods through me. "That's excellent news. Are you kidding me?"

"It is," he says, his expression faltering.

I narrow my gaze. "But?"

"But..." he pulls back, running his hand across the back of his neck. "My inheritance money won't cover as much as I originally thought. Even with the house sale, the county is taking a large chunk to recoup the costs for having the hospice services come out. So..." His voice trails off and he walks away.

"So...? What does that mean?" I repeat, standing up and following him.

"It means I'll just about have enough to cover a full year." His eyes drop to the floor and he presses his lips tight. "And that's it."

"Okay, well, that still gives you time. Right? I mean, that's not *terrible*."

He tilts his head to the side, shrugging. "I suppose. But it really just delays the inevitable. I either have a money problem now, or I have a money problem in a year."

"But in a year, a lot could change. You can apply for scholarships and grants in the meantime. If you get a part-time job, you could save up. There are options," I say, pressing my fingertips into the tabletop.

Wade steps forward, wrapping his arms around my shoulders. "Have I told you, I love your optimism?"

I press my cheek into his chest and pull him in tight. "Why do I get the impression that's your way of saying you've lost hope?"

"I'm not. I'm just a realist, Autumn. There's a good chance I won't be able to continue after this year," he says, stepping back. "I don't want to sugarcoat it and make it something that it's not."

I shake my head. "No, I refuse to accept that. There's gotta be something we can do between now and then."

"There is," he says plainly.

"What? Anything... Name it, let's do it," I say, my eyes wide.

"Come with me to the academy so I can give them my cashier's check for the year. Then, help make this year the most amazing one ever," he says, pushing a strand of my hair behind my ear.

He flashes me one of his trademark winks only he can manage.

I swallow hard. Can I do that? Spend the next year trying to forget that it might be his only year in the school? Or act like it's no big deal?

"*Please*, Dru?" he whispers, rubbing his thumb across my cheek. "I need this."

I sigh, dropping my gaze to the tabletop. "All right. Get your things."

He bends in, kissing the spot where his thumb just was. "Thank you," he breathes against my cheek.

I roll my eyes in defeat and stand up.

Twisting around, he walks over to the breakfast bar and grabs his keys and wallet. Then, he moves to the door and swings it open. "After you."

I tip my head, walking out the door and into the hallway, practically running straight into Chelsea.

"Sorry, dear. Had my head in the clouds," she says, wrapping her hands around my upper arms and steadying us both.

I shake my head. "No, it's my bad. I wasn't looking where I was going. I guess I sorta figured the hallway would be deserted."

"Fair dues, considering most of my tenants are introverts," she chuckles. Then her face suddenly turns dark and serious. "Hey, did you guys hear about what's happening in town?"

Wade steps out, locking the apartment door. When the lock clicks into place, he spins around and shakes his head. "Been holed up trying to get unpacked. What's going on?"

Chelsea looks to me and I shake my head as well. She leans in, clasping her hands together. "Someone's been digging up graves in town. And it's not the cemetery's gravedigger."

"What?" I practically snort. "Why would anyone do that?"

She shrugs. "Who knows? My money is on kids. There were two newly dug graves that were desecrated. The ground was completely dug up and the *bodies missing*." Her green eyes widen to the point of practically falling out of her head. Even though it's horrifying news, it's pretty clear she's enjoying the gossip of it.

"That's horrible," Wade says, his eyebrows tugging in.

"Well, yeah. But totally intriguing. I don't have internet, so it's one of the more exciting things I've heard around here," Chelsea says, laughing softly.

"Why do you think it was kids?" I say, circling back around to her original thought.

"Because the bodies were missing and they were both new graves. The earth was probably way softer, making it easier to dig up. I mean, do you know any kids willing to go out of their way to work? Especially for a practical joke or whatever they thought this was…"

"Maybe they were robbing the bodies. Sometimes people get buried with things," I say, trying to make sense of the vandalism.

"Nada. Neither one was buried with anything of value. The police wondered the same thing, according to Sheriff Gordon." She leans in, covering the side of her mouth with the back of her hand. "He's my cousin."

"Creepy," I say. "The grave robbing, that is. Not that the sheriff is your cousin."

Wade chuckles and nods.

"Well, he's pretty creepy, too. But yeah, they're at a bit of a loss. Should be interesting to see what happens when they find out who did it. Well, anyway, I didn't mean to stop you," Chelsea says, shooing us with her hands. "Go, go. I can see you were heading off somewhere. Hopefully, more exciting than this place." She smirks.

"Thanks," Wade says, tipping his head. "Let us know if you hear anything else, though."

"Oh, trust...if I hear anything, I'm coming straight for you," she laughs, wandering off down the hallway.

Again, a twinge of jealousy writhes its way into my abdomen. I twist around and start heading for the door, completely willing to brave the insane cold to escape the frigid feeling in here.

"Hey, woman. Hold up, would you?" Wade says, chasing after me. He slides his hand into mine and pulls me back as we get to the door. Without a word, he opens the door, so I can go through first, as always. The insanely cold air thrusts its way into the hall, making me shudder, but I ignore it.

"Thank you," I say, releasing his hand and sliding it along his waist as I go by.

He shudders. "Now, *that*, you can definitely do more often."

A smile spreads across my lips, melting some of the concerns. "Come on, mister. Let's get your money over to Ms. Cain." I tip my head toward my vehicle and start to race him. "I'll drive."

"I can hardly wait for the onslaught of elation to roll off Ms. Cain. It's bound to be epic," Wade says as he gets inside Big Blue.

I snicker under my breath and put the vehicle into drive.

The trip to Windhaven Academy takes less than five minutes from Wade's apartment. Had the day been warmer, it would even have been a nice walk. The parking lot is devoid of the usual hustle and bustle of student cars since the semester doesn't start until Monday. Instead, a small huddle of SUVs and Cadillacs in the faculty lot are the only clue the school has people inside.

"At least this should be fast," I say, pulling up as close as possible to the front door.

"I've seen Ms. Cain in action. When she's behind that desk of hers, nothing moves fast," he says, reaching for his handle.

I nod. "You're not wrong."

We make our way to the enormous school entrance as quickly as possible, but as soon as it's within reach, Wade stops to look up.

"Cool gargoyles," he says, pointing. "Never noticed those before."

My gaze follows his fingers and I smile. There are multiple gargoyles on the building, if you look close enough. But the ones he's pointing to are griffins, with what looks to be a large piece of rope dangling from their beaks.

"Pretty awesome, right?" I say, shivering from the cold.

He reaches for the door handle, nodding. "For sure. Come on, get inside before you turn into an Autumncicle."

As we step inside the school, the floor squeaks with each of our steps, clearly newly polished in preparation of Monday's fresh arrivals. Everything about the building sparkles, from the banisters on the large stairway to the windows and walls.

The door to Ms. Cain's administration office is wide open. As we enter, she looks up slowly, taking her time to cast her gaze out over the dark-rimmed glasses.

"Ah, Mr. Hoffman. So delighted to see you. I take it

this means you have some good news. Should I start jumping for joy?" Ms. Cain says, her tone dripping with sarcasm.

Wade nods, pulling out the cashier's check from his pocket and slides it across the space between him and Ms. Cain. "Well, it's good news, depending on how you look at it. But I have tuition covered."

She tips her head in acknowledgement. "Very well. Thank you, sir. I'll make sure your hold is lifted and you can continue on with classes as planned, come Monday morning. Do you require another copy of your schedule?"

"No, I'm good. I have it memorized already," he says, smiling broadly at her.

"Do you, now?" she says, quirking an eyebrow, clearly impressed.

"Yep, sure do. It wasn't that hard. There's only six classes to keep track of."

"You should teach that trick to your fellow classmates," she chuckles. "The sheer number of lost students I'll have to deal with this coming week already makes my head hurt."

"Well, you'll have one less to contend with. Have a lovely day," he says, laying his sweet on thick.

Ms. Cain smiles. "The two of you as well. Enjoy the rest of your weekend."

I cast a quick wave at her, and her smile twists into a smirk. Walking out behind Wade, I bump my shoulder into his. "What was all that?"

"All what?" he asks, arching an eyebrow and walking out the door.

"You sure impressed Ms. Cain back there. I don't think I've ever seen her quite so...*happy*." I narrow my eyes at him, unsure that happy and Ms. Cain belong in the same sentence.

He raises his eyebrows and shrugs. Leaning in, he whispers. "I learned a long time ago, you can never be too nice to the administrative staff. If they like you, doors open that may not have existed. They are the eyes and ears of their establishments, but everyone overlooks them."

My mouth drops open, and I stop my descent down the snow-covered stone steps. "Ah, that makes total sense. It's always been uncanny the way that woman can memorize people's names and faces without even having met them."

"Maybe that's her gift," Wade says, matter-of-factly.

I halt my progress to Big Blue, blinking back surprise. "You know, she's always seemed so mundane. It never occurred to me that she might have a special ability, too."

"She works at a supernatural school, Autumn. I think it's pretty safe to say everyone who works here has some sort of gift," Wade says, winking at me.

My heart beats faster and I reach for his hand.

Suddenly, the Lucifer theme song goes off, and Wade pulls up short, reaching for his phone in his back pocket. He eyes the phone number, raising an eyebrow, then eyeing me.

After a moment, he raises the phone to his ear. "Hello?"

His expression flits from confusion to concern as he swaps the phone from one ear to the other.

"Are you...are you sure?" he says.

Silence follows and I shiver in the cold, swapping which leg I put the most weight on. My gaze falls on Blue, just a few feet away, but I don't dare leave him standing here alone because he doesn't look thrilled. I wish I could read minds or hear what's going on with the other end of the call.

Wade's silver eyes darken, and he meets my expectant gaze. "Okay, thank you for letting me know. I appreciate it."

He hangs up the phone, staring blankly at me. The edges of his jaw tighten and release, but he doesn't say anything at first.

"What is it? Is everything okay?" I finally ask, unable to stand the suspense.

Wade's nostrils flare and his black pupils consume nearly all of the silver lining. "Not really."

I exhale a billowing breath. "What's happened?"

His eyebrows crumple inward and he stares absently at the phone in his hand. "Someone's broken the door on my grandpa's columbarium and stolen his cremains."

CHAPTER 5

RUMORS ON THE FIRST DAY

This new semester is already tainted by torment. Wade and I spent so much time apart last year, and now that we're finally together, living in the same town and going to the same school, in some ways, I feel more distant from him than ever.

He spent the entire weekend going back and forth to Mistwood Point to figure out what to do with his grandpa's columbarium and talking to the police. As much as I wanted to go with him, he insisted this was something he had to do on his own and I know it's tied to the strange conversation at the graveyard. I just can't prove it.

Now, here we are, first day back at school—his literal first day at Windhaven Academy—and I have no idea where he is.

I pull out my phone, staring at the lack of notifications, and sigh. Do I text him again? Or do I just go on with my day and hope he catches up with me?

I'll give him a few more minutes.

Shaking my head, I take a seat on the stone steps in

front of the school. Then, I spend the next five minutes fiddling with my phone, swapping it from hand to hand as I cast my gaze over the sea of students and their rides.

"I heard there was another robbing in a town south of us. Mistwood something or other," a dark-haired girl says to a small congregation of others as they make their way up the steps.

The rumor mill has already started. I don't know why I'm so surprised. Even supernatural people are still people.

Flipping my phone over, I check on the time. "Dammit," I mutter under my breath.

Standing up, I flip open my messages and shoot Wade a final quick text.

Heading inside. Hope everything's okay. Find me when you get a free minute. <3 Dru

I shut off the screen and cram it back into my pocket.

Inside the school, I catch snippets of multiple conversations, all centered around the grave robbings. Seems like everyone finds the act completely fascinating—or appalling. But either way, totally of their concern.

I shake my head, making my way to Intermediate Spellcasting alone. Thankfully, a semester in the building has made me as adept at finding my classes as Cat was on the first day. When I turn the final hall, there stands Wade outside my door, a single red rose in hand. His grin stretches from ear to ear as I approach.

"I thought you were never going to get here," he says, handing me the flower and kissing the side of my face.

I shake my head, holding the flower close. "I was waiting for you outside."

"Yes, but that didn't fit into my plan of surprise." The creases in the corner of his eyes deepen as his smile widens.

"You are a pain, you know that?" I say, shaking my head. "I have to get to class now and I totally missed you. I was hoping to have more time with you this morning and now you're going to be late."

He shakes his head. "No, I'm already here."

I snicker softly. "You don't have Intermediate Spellcasting."

"You're right, I don't," he says, narrowing his gaze. "I have Spellcasting Basics."

I tilt my head, confused.

"It's taught in the same classroom. Remember what Mrs. Arlo said at the Witching Stick? The classes are tailored for each student's level?" he says, smirking. "Yeesh, at least I paid attention."

Blinking back surprise, my mouth drops open. "Oh my gosh, you're right."

Wade tips his head to the doorway and holds out his elbow. "So, would you do me the honors of sitting next to me?"

"As if you'd be able to have it any other way." I loop my arm through his and together we walk inside.

Throughout the day, Wade and I end up having three of our six classes together, despite being taught at completely different levels. From class to class, I can't help but be awestruck as I look around the room, wondering what each student is actually hearing and how it's different from what lessons are being taught to me. It's brought a whole new level of fascination to the school and the way it operates.

On the strange side, I haven't seen hide nor hair of Cat and Colton, but it could just mean we have completely different schedules this year. Or perhaps, Cat needed to take an additional day or two to rest. It wouldn't be unheard of after all the exertion she must have expelled as tour guide.

When we reach the end of the day, Wade and I meet up in the commons to compare first-day notes. Unfortunately, his outgoing and easy attitude has vanished, replaced with his more withdrawn persona.

"Did school not go well?" I finally ask after ten minutes of silence, sitting together in the commons.

Wade glances up. "I—yeah, sorry. Was thinking."

"I noticed," I say, tapping the armrest on my chair. "Anything you want to talk about?"

His eyebrows tug in and he leans forward, resting his elbows on his knees. "Have you been hearing things? About me, I mean?"

Surprise flashes through me and I shake my head. "No. Why?"

He rubs his hand across his mouth. "I don't know. Maybe I'm being overly self-conscious, but I swear, I feel everyone's eyes on me. Like they're judging me for something, and I have no idea what."

"That's ridiculous. No one here knows you," I say.

He nods. "Right? That's what I keep telling myself, but I swear, there's a vibe..."

"I'm sure it's just first-day jitters. I felt the same way last year."

Two guys enter the commons, view the two of us, and stop. A tall, lanky brunette leans over to his blond friend and says, "That's the one."

Wade frowns, his jaw clenching.

"Hey," I say, standing up. "You got something to say?"

The shorter blond steps forward, tipping his chin toward Wade. "Yeah, why would you do that to your grandpa's grave? Cold, man."

"Yeah, like, I can't say I like my grandparents either but that's brutal," the other one says.

Wade's gaze narrows and before he can retort, the two guys twist around and head back the way they came.

"What in the hell?" I say, returning to my seat.

Wade's expression darkens. "Ah, they think I'm the one robbing graves. Excellent."

"No, I'm sure that's not..." I begin.

"You heard them, Autumn. At the very least, they think I damaged my own grandpa's columbarium. What in the actual hell? I thought when you went to a college people were meant to be smarter or *more mature*. It's like being in high school all over again," he says, leaning back in his chair. He blows out a long breath and looks up at the ceiling.

"Why on earth would anyone even tie those two things together? Your grandpa was cremated and the graves here were full-on graves with coffins. It makes no sense. The MO doesn't even match," I say, walking over to my chair and sitting back down.

Wade shrugs. "Probably because the two police teams feel like there are similarities."

"What?" I say, twisting to face him better. "There are?"

"Yeah, that's what they told me this weekend when I was in Mistwood. Magical signatures were found at both places, but that's as much as they know. Something about needing to bring in a special team to determine what kind of magic so they can clamp it down and figure out who it's tied to."

"Do they think you were involved?" I say.

Wade snickers. "I hope not. I don't have any magical abilities. At least, none that have surfaced yet. They're checking with the academy to verify, though. So much for being on Ms. Cain's good side."

My gaze falls to the ground. "Damn."

"Regardless, that obviously doesn't stop the gossip from spinning out of control. God, I wish I had a way to throw this all back in their faces. It's ridiculous." Wade runs his hands over his face. "One of the cops did say they thought it was similar to something that happened thirty some odd years ago. So, with a little luck, they'll be able to trace it back. Unless of course they think this is a copycat situation."

"Well, if it happened before, maybe we should take a trip to the academy library. Last semester, when I was trying to get clear on what was happening to me, going to the library was the only thing that kept me sane. Even though it didn't really feel like it at the time. I know it's a different library, but what I was searching for wasn't magical—at least, it didn't start out that way."

Wade quirks an eyebrow skeptically. "Why the library? There is this huge information superhighway called the *internet*. It also has the added bonus of not needing to be around people."

"Yes, but the supernatural underground isn't always broadcasting all of its news on the World Wide Web, he who wishes to hide," I say, smiling. "Besides, I could call Cat and have her meet us. She might know—"

Wade shakes his head, raising a hand. "No, I'd rather not involve Cat if we can avoid it."

I clamp my lips shut and nod.

"I didn't mean to be so abrupt. I like Cat, I really do," he says, backpedaling.

I wave a hand in front of me. "Don't worry about it. I get it."

"All right, if you think we could dig up something..." Wade's face scrunches. "That was *not* a Freudian slip. I swear it."

I chuckle. "You don't have to convince me, Wade. I know you wouldn't do anything like this."

He lets out a sigh of relief. "Good. I'd hate to think this sort of bullshit could shake your confidence in me. I just can't even believe it, you know?"

Standing up, I take a seat on his lap and wrap my arms around his neck. "I'm not a rumor girl. This doesn't shake my confidence in you. Not even a little bit. I know you, Wade Hoffman. But I wish you would open up to me more. We need to get on the same page again. So, come on, let's go see if anything like this has happened before. If magic is involved, we should be able to find something."

"I sure as hell hope so. This is not how I planned to spend my one and only year here," he says, frowning.

"Don't say that. We'll get that sorted out, too. But one thing at a time," I mutter, kissing the crease where his eye meets his cheekbone. "All right, let's do it." I stand up and reach out, offering my hand.

Together, we walk to the school's library. The space looks more like a place of worship than a place to learn and read things. Especially with its high ceilings and stained-glass windows that span the entire height of the room. However, the ambiance is unlike anything else.

In all honesty, I've only been in this library a handful of times and never to do research like this, so I feel a little out of sorts. All of my personal research last year was done at the local library in town—and in a dark corner of it, too.

"Where do we start?" Wade says, his wide eyes mimicking my own.

I shrug and point to the man behind the desk. "Ask the librarian?"

"All right, then, let's do it." He nods.

Walking forward, Wade makes his way to the large, round oak desk in the center of the main aisle. It's clear it's been set intentionally because it commands the space and draws you straight to it. The artistry in the wood carvings on the front is similar to the work in the admissions office, but instead of someone short and stout, a broad-shouldered man with dark hair and inquisitive eyes scrolls through an old-fashioned-looking library catalogue. On the desk, the nameplate reads: *David Chen*.

"Excuse me," Wade says, clearing his throat.

David glances up and grins. "Ah, Mr. Hoffman. It's a pleasure to meet you in person." His voice has a tinge of echo to it, and I turn to Wade, raising an eyebrow in surprise.

"I—uh, thanks?" Wade says, shooting me a sideways glance. "Say, I was wondering if you happen to have any information on, uh…" he pinches his lips tight for a moment. "Actually, you know what? Do you have a place to view any old magical news articles from thirty years ago or so?"

"What you're seeking is likely all online now, but I can point you to the public computer section," David says with a knowing smirk.

Wade again shifts his gaze to me, and I shrug sheepishly.

"No need, I can see it from here," Wade says, sliding his hand into mine and pulling us both to the right of the expansive room.

"See, told you. *Online*," he chuckles when we're out of earshot of the librarian.

"Okay, so you win this round," I say, taking a seat at one of the computers and glancing over my shoulder at the librarian. "Can I ask you something? Did the librarian's voice seem odd to you?"

"Yeah, kinda almost robotic," Wade says, nodding as he fiddles with the mouse to wake the sleeping computer.

"Right? You don't think that's a thing, do you?" I say, unable to stop myself from eyeing the desk.

Wade shrugs. "I don't see why not. I mean, you're a *necromancer*, for crying out loud. You think an AI is as crazy as it gets?"

"Point taken," I say, turning back around and facing the computer. "So, what's the game plan?"

"Well," Wade begins, letting his fingers fly across the keyboard, "the only thing I have to go on is what I heard in Mistwood. So, I guess we start by looking to see if there were any other grave robbings back in the late eighties or early nineties."

I groan. "This is gonna be like looking for a needle in a haystack."

Wade nods, but bends in. "Except...I found something."

My mouth drops open and I lean in, too. "You're kidding?"

"No, I'm just good with internet searches." He twists around and beams at me. "Get this. It says there were two graves desecrated, but that's not all. There were some weird vandalizations as well."

"Weird how?"

Wade leans in, reading a bit further.

"Scorched markings over the tops of some of the other freshly dug graves—days after the initial robbings. It was unique enough that it drew attention and witnesses saw someone with magical abilities at the scene," he finally says.

"Okay, that's strange and all, but I don't know—" I begin, but stop when Wade's jaw drops open and the color drains from his cheeks. "What is it?"

Shifting his gaze from the computer gaze to me, Wade leans back and presses his fingertips to his lips. His eyelashes flutter furiously as he processes whatever he just read.

"What is it?" I press.

"They had a suspect," he whispers.

"That's good. It means we can track down—"

Wade shakes his head. "It was my *dad*."

CHAPTER 6

ALL THAT FOLLOWS

I f anyone in school finds out about Wade's dad being the prime suspect in what happened thirty years ago, they'll have him tried and convicted before anyone can change their minds.

With both his dad and grandpa dead, there's no one in the family he can turn to in order to make sense out of this mess. And no one else the authorities can point fingers to, at least not as easily.

As I walk down the hallway to Grimoire Protection, my mind is too busy grappling with Wade's new dilemma to pay attention to my surroundings. I turn the corner and wind up tripping over my own two feet as the floor ascends upward in a gradual ramp. My books go flying as I reach out to break my fall.

"That was graceful," Cat chuckles, rushing up to me.

Colton follows closely behind her, his expression the epitome of shock.

"Wow, I guess I was lost in thought," I mutter, picking

up the two books that flew out of my arms and drawing them into to my chest as I stand up.

Cat's dark eyes crinkle at their edges. "And people wonder why *texting* and walking is a bad idea."

"Ha, ha. Very funny, smartass," I say, making a face. "It's good to see you guys. I didn't catch you at all yesterday. Where were you?"

"Ugh, don't get me started," Cat says, rolling her eyes.

"Something triggered the school's wards when we came in yesterday and they had to do some tests to make sure we weren't packing or whatever," Colt mutters, shaking his head.

"Weird," I say, scrunching my face.

Colton shuffles to his other foot, watching the floor with great intensity.

"So, is everything okay now? I mean, it must be if you're here," I say.

Cat nods tersely. "Yeah, all good. How was the first day for you?"

"Okay," I say, shrugging. "Weird."

Quirking an eyebrow, Cat says, "Weirder than us getting stopped at the door before we even make it to my first class?"

"Yeah, actually." I pull my phone out of my pocket to check the time. We still have five minutes before class starts. "Have you guys been hearing any...*rumors*? You might not if you were out of circulation yesterday."

"Like your boyfriend gets his kicks out of desecrating graves," Colton says, refusing to look up.

My shoulders drop. "Yeah, those kinds of rumors. They're not true, by the way."

Cat's face scrunches to the side and she says, "Are you totally sure? I mean, how well do you really know him?"

My back immediately bristles at her words. I clench my jaw and breathe slowly through my nose, trying to disperse my irritation. It's not their fault. They're only repeating what others are saying.

"I know him pretty damn well. He wouldn't do something like that," I mutter.

"Well, it happened in Mistwood Point, which is where he's coming from. And then it happened here, right after he moved. Seems like kind of a big coincidence, if you ask me," Colton says, finally chancing a glance at me.

Another flash of anger coils through my insides. "You don't know him at all. And besides, why desecrate his grandpa's grave, then come here and dig up two others? It doesn't make any sense."

"Maybe he was angry he didn't get the inheritance he expected," Cat says, shooting me an apologetic look.

"What?" I balk, shooting a glance between the two of them. "You've got to be kidding. First of all, where did you even hear this?"

"When we were being tested yesterday, I overheard Ms. Cain mentioning something to Professor Lambert," Cat says, looking over her shoulder at Colton.

"Wow. His finances are no one else's business. And just so you're aware, Wade did everything he could for his grandpa. He became a PCA just to be able to take care of him while he was dying," I say, channeling my anger through clenched teeth.

"Yeah, and where was he during all the time before he was on his deathbed? Ever ask yourself that? Seems pretty convenient that he swooped in at the end, if you ask me,"

Colton says, shrugging nonchalantly. "Cat, we should really get to class. I don't want to miss Organic Transmutation. We'll get to combine our elements in there and see what happens."

Cat nods, but turns to me with pity in her eyes. "We're just looking out for you, Autumn. I know you want to think the best of Wade, but maybe you need to ask yourself some difficult questions. And who knows? Maybe you're right. Maybe this is all just a misunderstanding. But if it's not..."

"I get it," I say, waving a hand and cutting her off.

"We really are just trying to help," Cat says, taking a few steps away from me, with Colton doing the same.

I turn back to the way I was heading and mutter under my breath, "Yeah, sure."

The rest of the day passes in a blur. Even though my last two classes are with Wade, neither of us is in much of a talkative mood. Plus, no matter how much I try to focus on my remaining classes, my mind keeps getting pulled back into the conversation with the twins.

What if they're right? Am I being naive and only seeing what I want to see about him?

I lean back in my seat for Advanced Life Energies, glancing over at Wade in the desk beside me. He's faced forward and looks like he's listening intently, but I'm sure his mind is still whirling, too.

Wade's been hiding details about his life from me and I've been letting him because of my own guilt. Maybe I should talk to him about some of the questions the twins brought up? If he has nothing to hide, surely he wouldn't mind answering.

Then again, if I do...will it upset him to learn it's

partially coming from Colton? And could it lead to another discussion about his interest in me?

Closing my eyes, I turn to face forward in my seat.

I wish I had someone else I could talk to who could make sense out of this. Someone who doesn't have a vested interested one way or the other.

My eyes pop open.

Abigail.

I'm surprised I didn't think of her sooner. In a strange way, after all of the help she provided with Cat's resurrection, she almost feels like another mother to me. Only, she's a mother who understands the supernatural and doesn't freak out at any mention of powers or abilities, the way my mom would.

With a little luck, my ghostly ancestor will have some insights I haven't considered. If nothing else, it would be nice to get another female perspective—one that's a little more sympathetic than Cat was today.

When class ends, I pick up my backpack and wait for Wade to gather up his things.

"Want to come over to my place to study?" Wade asks, standing up and walking around his desk.

I nod. "That sounds good. I have a few things I need to do quick at home. Can I meet you about six?"

"Sure, that works," he says, bending in and brushing his lips against my cheek.

A flurry of anxiety courses through my veins. I could kick myself for feeling so torn about Wade. But I also don't want to be that girl who refuses to think anything could be wrong with a guy just because she likes him.

"Do you want me to order pizza or anything? Or do

you plan to eat at home?" Wade asks, leading us out into the hallway.

"How about I bring something? Save your money," I say, reaching for his hand and giving it a squeeze.

His expression falters, but he nods.

"I'm sorry, I didn't mean anything by that," I sputter.

"It's okay, I get it," Wade says, shaking his head.

Biting my lip, I opt for walking silently beside him. Rather than heading to the Commons for a few minutes, we head straight out the door and to our vehicles. At least today, we arrived at nearly the same time, so we're parked together.

When we reach our rides, I lean up against the side of Blue and turn to face Wade. "You know, we really should start riding together."

"I don't want you to feel like you're stuck here, though. I mean, if you ever have to leave early or anything..." Wade says, shaking his head.

"Don't be ridiculous. Besides, I'd mostly know in advance and we could coordinate then," I say, narrowing my gaze. "Why don't you want to ride with me?"

Wade chuckles, "It's not that at all."

"Then what is it?"

"Honestly, I have no idea. I guess I'm so used to being apart, I don't want to suffocate you," he says, shrugging sheepishly. "Stupid, right?"

"Not at all," I say, reaching for his waist and pulling him close. "But from now on, we're riding together. Deal?"

"Yes, ma'am." He chuckles.

"Since you're closer to the school, I'll come to you," I say glancing up just in time to see him open his mouth in protest. "*No arguments.*"

His lips pinch shut.

"Promise me," I say.

"Fine," he mutters through clenched teeth.

"All right, now that that's settled, I'm going to head home. I'll see you at six," I say, standing on my tiptoes and pressing my lips to his.

Surprisingly, he bends in, pressing his body against mine until he pins me against the side of Blue. The force of his kiss takes my breath away and I raise my right hand, entwining my fingertips into his dark hair.

"Get a room," someone yells out beside us.

We separate out of surprise and I turn to see Dominic jabbing his index finger into his mouth.

Wade's entire body goes rigid under my touch and his face pinches tight. The last time the two of them were in the same space, Dominic told him *his kind* shouldn't be anywhere near me.

I still have no idea what any of that was about, come to think of it.

"We better get outta here," Wade says, refusing to move his gaze from Dominic until he's gotten into his vehicle and driven off.

Nodding, I reach for my handle and get inside. I roll down the window and lean out for one more kiss. "See you in a bit."

"See ya," he says, pressing the palm of his hand against my cheek.

I pull out of the parking lot, keeping my eyes on the rearview mirror. Wade stands beside his car until I turn the corner and can no longer see him at all.

Sighing to myself, I head home on autopilot.

How is it possible to have such opposing thoughts and

feelings warring inside me at the same time? On one hand, I trust Wade with my life. On the other hand, I can see where Cat and Colt are coming from as well.

When I get home, I park in the middle of the big loop, right beside the large weeping angel statue. Leaving my backpack on the passenger seat, I head straight for the front door. The house is relatively quiet as I open the door and walk into the main entryway. Rather than call out for my dad, the way I normally would, I make my way to my bedroom.

As I enter the space, I turn back and close my bedroom door as quietly as possible. I don't know why I feel the need to be sneaky about this, but it's been a while since Abigail appeared to me. It also doesn't help that a part of me feels like this is an idiotic reason to summon her.

When I turn around to face my bedroom, Abigail stands beside the large picture window, gazing out over the courtyard. It's almost as if she sensed my request before I sent it.

"Abigail?" I say, stepping into the middle of my room.

Turning around, her gown flows ethereally at her feet. It simultaneously touches the ground and doesn't, which somehow seems completely normal.

I take a moment to consider my questions. Finally, I let go of a deep breath and say, "There are some strange things happening and I could use your advice. I don't have anyone else I can really talk to about it."

Her expression softens and she smiles. Silently, she clasps her hands together in front of her body and waits.

Glancing down, I take a seat on the end of my bed. "Some graves have been desecrated in both Windhaven and Mistwood Point. Rumors are flying around the academy in town and people think Wade had something to do with it. At first...I thought they were being ridiculous. But, now I'm not so sure."

Abigail tips her head to the side and floats forward. "How exactly were the graves desecrated?"

I bite my lip. "Bodies were dug up. Well, here, at least. In Mistwood, the columbarium for Wade's grandpa was damaged and his urn removed."

"And why do you believe the two are intertwined?" she asks, listening intensely.

"Because the police do. They think magic was involved," I offer.

After a moment's contemplation, Abigail asks, "Have the bodies been recovered?"

I shake my head. "Not so far."

"I suggest proceeding with caution. I would not presume to suggest who or what is doing this horrendous act, but it is our duty to protect the dead. Not just raise them," she says, her voice tapering off.

"What do you mean?"

"If the dead are being desecrated, as you have said, the time has come for you to become versed in your gifts, Autumn. More than what any school may be able to teach on this subject," she says softly.

"Okay, and how exactly do I go about doing that? It's not like information is super-forthcoming. Plus, Dad's not around much to ask. And you're not exactly the epitome of straightforwardness," I say, frustration building.

"I wish I was of the living; it would make things far easier for you. I'd always wished to train a daughter," she says with a tone mixed with sorrow and nostalgia. "Begin by learning more about the manor and its location. My energy to corporealize wanes quickly, so I am but a guide, pointing the way. However, trust that the manor is the key. It will help you unearth what could be headed your way," she says. Her essence begins to flicker and she reaches out, trying to capture my attention. "Trust in this—if the bodies are not found and laid to rest, much worse things are sure to follow."

CHAPTER 7

NEW DOORS BEST LEFT CLOSED

I stare out the passenger window of Wade's car, watching the dead-looking trees and snow mounds drift by. My mind circles around the questions plaguing us the past week like the snow devils spinning alongside the road.

Who would vandalize the graves in both Windhaven and Mistwood Point? Why would they take the bodies from some, and the ashes of others? There's now been a total of seven graves desecrated, one in Windhaven and three more in Mistwood.

While no one has found Wade's grandpa's urn yet, the cemetery has been able to replace the door to his columbarium. I didn't realize just how much having it broken was weighing on Wade until he asked me to join him. He'd nearly broken down as he told me and I'm not sure if it was from the relief to have that part taken care of—or the overwhelm from dealing with everything the past week. Maybe both?

Twisting in my seat, I reach out and take his hand in mine. "Thank you for bringing me with you."

He gives my hand a squeeze, then lifts it to his lips. "Thank you for coming with me."

"Of course. Where else would I be, silly?"

"You could have said no," he says, shooting me a sideways glance. "I'm sure you have just as much homework as I do."

"And yet, it's still not as important as being there for you," I say, shooting him a smile.

His cheeks mound as he turns to face the road. "It's been an odd week, for sure. Nothing like what I expected. Hell, I wouldn't even blame you for wanting to keep your distance from me, you know."

My solar plexus clenches. "Don't be ridiculous."

"Still," he says, shrugging. He flips on his blinker and takes the next left into the cemetery.

I shake my head, sitting up straighter and looking around. Despite the recent bout of new vandalism, there's no immediate evidence of it as we pull in. The cemetery looks as pristine and serene as usual, thanks in part to last night's snowfall.

Wade pulls us up to the columbarium, parking in front of the large wall of concrete cubes.

"So far so good, huh?" he says, removing the key from the ignition and dropping his hand to his lap. His eyes sweep the graveyard, just like I had.

I nod. "I can't even tell anything unusual was going on. Can you?"

"Nope, everything looks *five by five*," he says, unbuckling his seatbelt and getting out of the car.

I follow after him, staying a foot or two behind so he

can be the first one to check out the new door. However, when he's a few feet away, he turns around and reaches his hand out. Smiling, I take it and stand beside him.

"Looks exactly as it should be," Wade whispers after a few moments. "They didn't change the style or anything."

"I was thinking the same thing."

"Too bad he's no longer in there. I still can't get my mind wrapped around that. Like, why would anyone want to do something like this? Damage graves. Mess with the dead. There are grieving families mixed into all of this. It's not just some funny prank," he says, taking a few steps back. He dusts off the snow from the same granite bench we sat on when his grandpa's ashes were laid to rest, then sits down.

I walk over, taking a seat beside him and sliding my hands between my knees. "I don't know. Whoever they are, they obviously weren't thinking about that. And if they were...well, it makes them kind of horrible in my book."

"Mine, too." Wade nods, taking a deep breath and dropping his gaze.

"So, what next? Is the cemetery going to increase security or anything?"

Wade shakes his head. "I don't think that's in their budget. As it is, the guys digging the graves around here are just people at the church down the road, who happen to know how to run a backhoe."

My eyes widen and I stare out in front of me. "Oh. Well, that's not very promising, then."

"Tell me about it. At this point, I'd be better off dawning spandex and a cape and trying to capture the bad guys myself," he snickers under his breath.

Flashes of him in tight leggings and a cape flash through my mind and my midsection erupts in butterflies. "Well, it certainly wouldn't hurt to give it a try. As long as I can watch."

A surprised laugh escapes his lips. "I'll do some digging to see what I can find."

"Oh, I'm sure they have superhero costumes down at the local clothing store," I say, keeping my face forward as warmth takes over my cheeks.

He shoots me a sideways glance. "I'll keep that in mind."

After a few moments of comfortable silence, I turn to him and say, "I know this whole thing has been hard on you. It's nice to see a little more of your normal self coming back."

Wade's dark eyebrows tug in and he nods. "Yeah, I've felt a bit out of sorts. It's hard enough dealing with death, but then all the other stuff...it's been kinda crazy. Plus, I definitely wasn't expecting the level of scrutiny I've been met with the first couple of weeks of school. You know?"

"I can imagine." I bite my lower lip, trying to decide if I should darken the subject by telling him about my conversation with Abigail and some of the concerns I have. Instead, I stand up, walking a few feet away from the columbarium so I can scan the tombstones. "Where do you think the latest grave robbings were?"

Wade follows me. "I dunno. I only heard they were fresh graves, just like the last time."

"Do you want to go look for them?" I ask, letting curiosity get the better of me.

Wade narrows his gaze. "Mmmm, I don't think that's probably the best of ideas. I mean, people already think

I'm guilty. The last thing I'd need is someone snapping a picture of us at the desecrated graves."

"Oh, good point. I'm sorry, I should have thought of that," I say, wiping my hand over my face.

"It's okay. I don't know why it would occur to you," he says, glancing around the rest of the cemetery. "You're not the one they're targeting."

"It should have. I guess I just don't believe all the rumors, so it didn't even occur to me that someone else might take advantage. It's not how my brain works."

Wade bends in, kissing the side of my neck. "And that's why I love you so much. You have such a good heart."

My stomach rolls and I frown. "Wade, I have to tell you something..."

His eyes widen slightly as he turns to look at me. Concern is clearly written across his features.

"It's nothing bad. At least, I don't think it is..." I say, straightening my shoulders. Immediately I opt then and there to only bring up one thing. "The other day, when you found out your dad was involved with something similar to this...I went home and summoned Abigail."

"All right..." he says, his silver eyes scrutinizing my every move.

"She thinks we need to be cautious," I say, fiddling with my pinkie. "She also seems to think the bodies need to be found. It was a pretty ominous message, actually."

Wade's eyes narrow and he asks, "Did she say anything else? You know, less cryptic?"

I nod. "She also said something about needing to understand my gifts more. That I'm here to protect the dead, not just raise them. She thinks I should do some digging into the manor, but I don't really know where to start. I mean, the library had some information, but I got the distinct impression what I need to know won't be found there."

"So, what about your dad? Could you ask him?"

"That's the plan. He's just been super-busy lately. Between him being gone and me being with you...finding a time when we're both home has been a challenge."

"Well, make it a priority to connect with him. Abigail hasn't steered you wrong so far. If she thinks there's something important about the manor, you probably want to figure out what it is," he says, reaching for my hand.

I take a deep breath, feeling better for having told him that piece. It's like a weight has been lifted and in the spirit of truthfulness, I grab hold of his hand, giving it a squeeze. Perhaps I could draw some truthfulness out of him.

"Wade, I really want to talk about that guy I saw you talking with the last time we were here," I say, exhaling slowly.

Wade quirks an eyebrow.

"Like I told you, when Cat and Colton had their accident...something strange happened. When the Vodník was destroyed and the souls were released...a man came. The same man I saw talking to you. Obviously, I don't know who he is, but he was going to take Cat's soul and I wouldn't let him. He threatened me, saying he'll be back. That I had no place meddling with things."

Wade's shoulders stiffen and his eyebrows tug in. Releasing my hand, he takes a step away from me, opting instead to stare at the columbarium.

"Wade, look, I know you were lying before about knowing him; I just don't know why. There's more going on here than you're letting on and I don't know why you're hiding it. I wish you'd just talk to me. I promise, I won't be mad. I just want to know what's going on," I say, walking up and reaching for his arm.

He lets me hold onto him, but refuses to say anything at first. His eyes rest on the large concrete structure looming in front of us.

Finally, he exhales, gently placing his right hand over mine. "Autumn, you're right to look for information. Especially after—" His gaze drops to my expectant eyes and he lets his fingertips graze against my cheek. "The thing is, I'm not sure what I can tell you."

I narrow my gaze, leaning into his touch. "I don't understand. Why can't you just open up about it? Are you —is he threatening *you*?"

Wade snickers under his breath, and he shakes his head. "No, it's nothing like that."

"Then tell me. Who is he? Why would he come to collect the souls? Is he like the Grim Reaper or something? What's really going on here?" I say, searching his eyes for comfort and answers.

"To be honest, I'm surprised you can even see him. And those who do usually forget after a few days. But I suppose that's neither here or there," he says, chewing on the side of his lip. "Ah, the hell with it. I'll tell you, but you have to promise me—"

A strange, scratching noise behind the columbarium makes him pause. Twisting around, I follow his gaze, but there's nothing there.

"What was that?" I whisper, holding tightly to Wade's arm out of surprise.

He shakes his head. "I dunno."

"Do you think someone's watching us? Oh god, what if you're right? Is there someone here taking pictures to incriminate us?" I say, suddenly concerned.

"Stay here. I'll check it out," he says quietly, holding an arm out and taking a tentative step forward.

"Not a chance, *Angel*. We go together. I've seen enough horror movies to know you never split up when there are strange noises," I say, shaking my head.

He shoots me a smirk, but nods. "Fine, but stay behind me. Deal?"

"I can handle myself," I say, jutting out my chin.

"Fine, together, then," he whispers, rolling his eyes in defeat.

Together, we take slow, deliberate steps forward, inching our way to the side of the columbarium. The sunlight is dwindling as it sets behind us and casts deep grooves on the small mounds of snow at our feet.

Before we reach the back of the columbarium, the scraping sound erupts again, and a man stumbles out from behind the structure. His clothes are tattered, and his skin is an awful shade of grey. Clumps of hair are even falling out of the top of his head.

Stumbling backward, I cover my mouth to keep from screaming. "What is that thing?" I squeak.

Before Wade can answer, the creature turns its empty eye sockets in our direction and races straight for us.

CHAPTER 8
UNDEAD THINGS

W ade spins around on his heel, grabbing hold of my arm as we run the opposite direction. Behind us, the creature lets out an ear-piercing screech and it surges forward, trying to keep up with us.

Before we can make it to the car, another zombie-like woman blocks our escape. She races out, coming between us and the vehicle. Her marble-grey hair is missing from one side of her head, and the skin on the left side of her face is beginning to flake away. Yet, just like the other one, her sunken eyes and missing eyeballs are the most horrifying part about her.

"This way," Wade commands, switching directions and heading toward the older part of the cemetery.

I follow him without question, my eyes scanning for a place to hide or a way to get away. Unfortunately, there are only gravestones, fake flowers and wreaths, and dormant trees—most of which have no low-hanging branches to grab onto. There are no buildings or even mausoleums to escape into.

"What do we do?" I cry out, my voice cracking as I struggle to maintain my momentum. The cold air makes my lungs hurt, but I keep running despite it.

"We need to find a better defense position," Wade says, scanning the area but refusing to stop running. I'm sure he's come to the same conclusion I have.

There's nowhere to run.

The two undead creatures pick up speed behind us, squealing like pigs about to be slaughtered. The sound is terrifying, and I clap my hands over my ears, trying to drown it out.

My legs begin to falter, and panic starts to bleed into every cell of my body.

"Whatever we do, we have to do it soon. I can't keep this up much longer. My quads are gonna give out," I cry.

I no sooner say the words than my left ankle rolls in a small dip hidden by the snow. The resounding crack and shot of pain that zips up my leg instantly pulls at my impulse to gag. Before I know it, I lose contact with Wade's hand and go down. I'm planted face first on the snowy ground, my leg throbbing from the knee downward. I bend forward, clawing at my leg as if it will somehow help.

Wade scrambles back to me, groping at my arms. "Come on, come on, Autumn." He does his best to yank me back onto my feet. "We have to keep moving. I don't know how to stop them. We have no weapons or anything."

I scream out in pain as I'm pulled upright. "I can't—I can't run. I've twisted something. It might be broken."

Panic swells inside me and the horror of the situation crashes down like an entire building being demolished. We're done for.

I'm done for.

"You need to go—" I yell, trying to push him away. "Get out of here."

Without even arguing with me, Wade scoops me up into his arms and trudges forward as fast his legs can carry us. Unfortunately, within seconds, the creatures close the distance. They reach out, tugging at the bottom of Wade's leather jacket and throwing him off balance. He stumbles forward, trying to set me down gently, but instead, he ends up dumping me into a small snow pile before he goes down as well.

I scramble back, doing my best to ignore the blinding pain as I try to put distance between myself and the haunting remnants of what used to be people. The rotten woman chases after Wade; the other decides I'm his, with his rotting fingers reaching out for me as I scramble back.

Twisting around, Wade kicks wildly at the creature as she drops to the ground, following his descent. Despite having no eyes to see with, they both have surprisingly quick reflexes. They crawl after us with fervor, dodging any attempts we throw at them to keep them at bay. Wade kicks vehemently as the bony fingers wrap around his ankle.

"Autumn, grab me the wreath stand," Wade yells, pointing to a freshly placed wreath a few yards away.

Scrambling to my feet, I half-crawl, half-hop to a wreath stand a couple of feet away. I pluck the wreath from it and fling it aside. Then, I hobble as close as I dare and hurl the stand in Wade's direction like a javelin. It misses him by a foot or two, but he manages to plant a forceful kick straight in the face of the undead woman. The impact removes the rest of her flesh, exposing her skull down to the bare bone. Luckily, it's enough of a hit for him to break free and crawl to the side to retrieve it.

As he swings back around, the male zombie shifts gears and takes the opportunity to go after Wade as well. He clutches at Wade's jeans, trying to make his way up the leg. Wade shifts the wreath stand in his grip, aiming the pointed end that would ordinarily plant into the ground, toward the creature. With absolutely no fear to stop it from advancing, the man continues to lurch forward, groping for Wade with terrifying fingers. Without hesitation, Wade thrusts the metal stand directly into his eye sockets.

Following the momentum from the creature as it lunges forward, Wade hoists him up and over, using his right leg to give himself more leverage. The dead man lands in the snow behind him with a sickening crack, but it doesn't regain animation.

The female, on the other hand, reaches out and grabs Wade's foot. Her grasp must be insanely strong, as she yanks hard and drags Wade across the snow like a rag doll. His arms go up and over his head as he twists and turns, trying to grab onto anything to break free. Finally, Wade bends forward and clutches at her bony fingers, pulling off chunks of flesh with each attempt to make her release his foot.

Without thought, I limp over to the motionless creature a few feet away and try to pull the wreath stand from its head. I bite down on my lip to avoid screaming out in pain, but it's no use. The steel is embedded deep into the other side of the bone and refuses to let loose.

"Dammit," I curse, twisting around to see if I can find another one—or at least something like it.

Unfortunately, being in the older part of the cemetery means fewer people paying their respects through decorations. The closest wreath stand, or anything moveable for that matter, is far beyond my ability to grab it and get myself back to help.

Making the split-second decision to head into the fray, I limp over as close I dare and yell, "Hey, this way—you don't want him. Come here." I wave my hands wide, trying to draw her attention my way.

The creature pauses long enough to look in my direction but doesn't change its trajectory. However, the distraction is enough for Wade to plant a fierce kick to her wrist. With a deafening crack, the brittle joint severs, leaving her hand still clutched onto his boot but no longer attached to her wrist. Scrambling backward, he clambers to his feet and races in my direction, with the zombie seconds behind. She moves decisively, completely ignoring the fact that she has only one hand.

"Quick, behind that headstone," Wade yells, pointing to a large piece of granite to my left.

The thing is massive, nearly as tall as I am, but it offers little in the way of protection. I have no idea what he thinks we'll accomplish hiding behind it, but regardless, we both race toward it.

I hobble-run as fast as I can, but the pain is almost debilitating. As we come up on the tombstone, I skitter to a quick turn, and my footing gives out again. I plummet into the snow, rolling sideways in a totally ungraceful maneuver. Wade is nowhere in sight, but the zombie is on me in seconds, dropping to the ground as it latches onto my thighs with its leftover hand and stump.

Scurrying backward, I try to get far enough away so I can stand, but the creature claws at my legs, digging in and pulling herself farther up my body with her good hand. Biting my lip, pain tears through my right ankle from both the sprain and the bony fingertips as they bear down on my flesh. With my good foot, I rear up, kicking down as hard as I can at the place between her neck and shoulder. The momentum is enough to loosen her grip as she skitters down my leg and nearly falls off.

A loud, thumping sound reverberates through the otherwise-still cemetery. It starts off low, but then starts to grow louder until a grinding sound takes its place. Terror rises, as does a scream in the back of my throat, as I try to get upright and see what's causing the sound.

Somewhere close by, Wade yells, "Get out of the goddamn way."

Using all the remaining strength I have in my left leg, I plant another kick on the creature's face and struggle completely out of her grasp. I no sooner pull back my legs than an enormous granite headstone comes crashing down onto the zombie's outstretched form. The weight of it flattens her upper torso, severing her head from the rest of her body. It rolls forward unceremoniously and lands face-up in the snow.

Shuddering away the adrenaline, I scoot back another foot or two for good measure. No matter what I do, I can't seem to break my gaze away from the severed head.

"How did you know that was going to work?" I say,

clutching at my chest and sucking in large gulps of frigid oxygen.

Wade plops down into the snow, knees first, then drops onto his back, gasping for air. After a moment he says, "Years of watching *way* too much TV."

I stay seated upright, scanning the graveyard for any more signs of moment. At first, everything is all calm and quiet, but suddenly, the dead body in front of me begins to turn a strange ashen color. Large chunks of it begin to break apart, disintegrating from the bone until all that remains is a pile of remnants that no longer resemble a human at all.

"What the—?" I sputter, narrowing my gaze.

Wade sits upright, instantly alert. "What is it?"

I outstretch my arm, pointing to where the zombie had just been. "It's...gone. How can it be gone?" Shifting to my knees, I crawl on all fours to get a better look. I reach out and poke my index finger into the ashes and they continue to fade away, as if the molecules themselves are being erased from existence.

"How in the hell?" Wade says, suddenly by my side. "How is this possible?"

I shake my head. "Your guess is as good as mine. I'm in totally new territory here."

"Can you see the other one? Did it disintegrate, too?" Wade asks, pushing up to a stand.

"I can't see anything, so maybe it did. Help me up and we can go look together," I say, holding out my hand.

Furrowing his brow, Wade grabs hold of my hand and yanks me to my feet.

"I don't know what's going on here, but one thing I do know is, we have to get outta this cemetery before anyone sees the mess we've caused," Wade says, frowning. "The last thing I need is more rumors. Besides I'd hate to have you dragged into all of the conspiracy theories."

Scanning the graveyard, it only takes a moment to realize he's right. There's a large trail of disruption leading from the columbarium all the way to our location.

"Yeah, we better go. We'll have to do some research when we get back to Windhaven. This is definitely not the place for specula—"

In the distance, my periphery catches movement and I home in on it. I squint, trying to get a better view, but I can't quite make it out. Suddenly, the movement sweeps in front of the large brick wall at the edge of the cemetery. Dressed from head to toe in white, it becomes glaringly obvious that it's a person.

"What is it? What do you see?" Wade asks, stepping up beside me.

"Did you see that?" I say, refusing to even blink until the person is no longer in view.

"See what?"

I take a deep breath, finally looking Wade's direction. "You were right to be concerned. There was someone in the cemetery with us."

CHAPTER 9
A HOME FOR THE DEAD

I might be supernatural, but even that doesn't prepare a person for coming face to face with zombies. Real, flesh-falling-off, scary-as-all-hell... *zombies.*

The thing is, even with all the stuff I've learned at school, zombies have never come up. And I've been learning a lot of stuff about my craft and my abilities. You'd think it would be a pretty big deal.

Hobbling over to the computer section of the Wind-haven Academy library, I take a seat at one of the computers and cast a sideways glance to Wade. "How is it zombies are real, but they've never come up in our course-work? It's like no one wants to talk about them."

"We're also kind of newbies to this whole school thing. As much as we've seen, we can only consume so much information at once. I'm sure there's info out there—we just gotta know where to look," Wade says, sliding into the chair beside me.

I nod, bending down and rubbing at my pulsing ankle. "Thus, the library."

"How's your leg?" Wade asks, quirking an eyebrow.

"I'll live. It just aches a bit," I mutter, setting my hand in my lap. The truth is, it's painted a lovely shade of black and blue, but at least I can walk on it now.

"Good." Wade says, eyeing me suspiciously before turning back to the computer. "The way I figure it, there's probably a lot of stuff out there we don't know about. But if we can dream it up, it probably exists. I mean, the ideas for some of the modern entertainment stuff, like zombies, had to have come from somewhere. Don't you think?"

"Good point," I say, turning to the computer screen. Quickly, I enter my login details to get into the school's vast archives of the magical, paranormal, and straight-up supernatural. After a few seconds, the search bar pops up and I quickly type in "zombies," then press enter.

Wade leans in, placing his left hand on my right thigh as we wait. It doesn't take long before the results come back.

"There's only four," I say, making a face. "Does that seem right to you?"

"That does seem odd," Wade says, narrowing his gaze. "Open the first one."

I click on the link and it opens a small landing page with a reroute.

Zombies > see also Revenants.

We exchange a glance, but I click on the link for Revenants. Something about the word reminds me of a conversation I had last semester, but I can't remember who it was with.

As the first page loads, I read the details out in a hushed voice, "Revenants are animated corpses and/or remains that have been revived from death to haunt the living. The word *revenant* is derived from the Old French word, *revenant*, meaning the 'returning.' See also the related French verb *revenir*, meaning 'to come back.' Instances of revenants, both in name and in reality, have declined since the 1700s. This is believed to be thanks to the rise in scientific exploration, as well as the implementation of supernatural schools across the United States. Academies, such as the Windhaven Academy in Massachusetts, channel supernatural talents in a constructive manner, avoiding some of the darker elements of magic, such as revenants."

"Well, I guess this explains why we haven't heard much about them," Wade mutters, shifting back in his seat.

"Yeah, for starters, everyone uses a different name," I say, chewing on the side of my lip.

"Yeah, but I've never heard of revenants. Have you?" Wade chuckles. "I mean, there was that one movie with Leo DiCaprio—but that wasn't even about zombies. Granted, he was kinda left for dead..."

"I must have missed that one," I say, shaking my head. "Well, okay, so basically, we know zombies can happen—but we don't really know why or how."

"Obviously, someone's behind it. It says they're revived to haunt the living. So, spellwork has to be involved in it."

"Who in the world would want to do something like this?" I say, unable to hide the disgust in my voice. It just seems ludicrous to me.

"Someone with an agenda...and the power to pull it off," Wade says, crossing his arms over his chest.

"Should we go to the police? I mean, tell them what happened to us in the cemetery the other day? Now that we know this part, maybe they can help?" I offer.

Wade looks doubtful as he places a curved hand over his mouth. "I dunno. I'm really torn about it. People already think I'm involved. If we go to the police, even the supernatural ones, will it just bring more suspicion? It says there, it's a darker element of magic. What if there are laws against this sort of thing."

"But you're innocent. That has to stand for something, right?"

Wade sighs, running the back of his hand across my jawline. "And that's why I love you so much. You really do think everything works out in the end."

"You don't?" I say, quirking an eyebrow.

"I want to," he says, his eyebrows flicking upward. "I'm just more realistic than that. Good people get hurt. Bad people sometimes win. When you bring in the supernatural, I'd wager those odds go up."

"Why do you say that?"

"Because power corrupts," he says, casting me a knowing look and standing up. "Having abilities, no matter how slight, can give a person a superiority complex. Especially if they're already a tad on the unstable side. Don't you think?"

"Yeah, I guess."

Wade looks up at the clock on the wall. "Lunch is nearly over. We better get moving. I don't want to miss Powers and Technology. It's been a good class so far. You coming?"

I nod, glancing quickly at the screen. "Yeah, I'll be there in just a minute. I want to do a little more reading on revenants, and I'll head out. Postmortem Communication isn't far from here."

Wade bends in, brushing his lips against mine. "Okay, meet you in an hour?"

"Sounds like a plan," I say, grinning.

He saunters out, walking through the library like he owns the place. Despite all the craziness going on around him, he still has such magnetism and an air of confidence about him.

Running my hand along my neck, I twist around to face the computer. Hitting the back button, I click on the next two links. They have all the same information as the first one, with small variations.

The fourth link, however, goes into the details between the mindless undead and those with independent, cognizant thought. Revenants are controlled by an outside force. *Liches* on the other hand, can somehow retain their minds—even when the rest of them has been desiccated.

I shudder at the thought of skeletal remains wandering around, somehow retaining their ability to think and make decisions. The mindlessly controlled ones are scary enough.

Leaning back, I stare blankly at the screen.

Why would anyone want to raise the dead and turn them into revenants? So far, what have they accomplished, other than launching a local investigation and causing suspicion to be thrown around?

My eyes widen.

What if whoever has been raising the dead has deliberately sent the revenants to *Wade*? And if that's true, why?

It doesn't make any sense.

Taking a deep breath, I turn back to the computer. Abigail told me that if the dead weren't found and laid to rest, worse things would follow. It's pretty clear now, she meant they'd become revenants. So, my guess is, this sort of thing has happened before.

I tap my fingertips on the edge of the keyboard, thinking.

She also mentioned, I need to do some research on the house in order to get a better picture of what's going on. Abigail and Warren were part of the founding of Windhaven but I'm not sure how it all ties back to Blackwood Manor.

Biting my lip, I put the cursor in the search bar and type *Blackwood Manor*. I fully expect for it to come up with a big fat nothing, especially after having to go to the county library to get more information last semester. However, that's not the case. Nearly sixty results come back.

Scanning through them quickly, the majority of them are focusing on the house and its relationship to the energy of the town. Eyeing the time, I frown.

Do I race to Postmortem Communication? Or do I stay here and dig a little deeper?

"Ah, screw it. It's one day," I whisper, returning my gaze to the computer screen "Besides, this way, I can get more information out of Abigail later."

I click on the first article, bending in to see exactly what kind of information a school would keep on my house. Of course, the piece is small, but talks about the house and its unique location. Evidently, people believe it was built on a vortex of energy—like a gateway that makes it easier to see and summon the dead.

Maybe that explains why my abilities didn't present themselves until I was there? Clicking through the next few links, the majority of the articles talk about the house and the way it was a beacon for those with supernatural abilities. In a way, it served as a stake in the ground, giving silent permission to those with power to join forces.

From the moment Abigail and Warren broke ground, other families with abilities were drawn to Windhaven, building their homes nearby. The Gilberts and the Cranes —Dominic's family—were the most notable.

Scanning the next page of results, one catches my eye and looks promising. I pull my seat in closer and give it a click.

August 26, 2005

Blackwood Manor's Magical Memory
Written by: Alexander Dunham

Windhaven, Massachusetts, is known for its supernatural draw, thanks to the Windhaven Academy and its magical teachings. Every year, thousands of supernatural hopefuls enroll into the elite super-school, hoping to learn how to master their gifts and become an even stronger version of themselves. However, hidden in the woods of Windhaven is a manor with a magical history all its own. Yet its significance seems to have been lost amongst the new generation of witches, shifters, and other magic-wielders.

Blackwood Manor is residence for one of the oldest families in Windhaven, the Blackwoods. Built in the 1700s, it was thought to be erected on hallowed ground in order to work in relationship with the Blackwoods's innate abilities. Both Warren and Abigail Blackwood were known for possessing strong powers in the post-mortem realm, gifts that were rare then and even more rare now. Together, they were a formidable team. Warren could both see and hear the deceased, making it easier to communicate with the dead. Abigail, on the other hand, was born a necromancer, with the ability to summon the souls of those who had passed and, under the right circumstances, bring them back to life.

Unfortunately, Abigail met an untimely death herself and her loss drove Warren into madness. He began creating additional rooms in the home at a feverish pitch. Those close to the family believed it was to make rooms for all of the children they would have liked to have had. However, in talking with the current descendant living in the home, Mr. Lyle Blackwood, he paints a very different picture.

"I think it would be a special kind of hell being able to see and hear spirits, but not being able to bring them back—especially when the one who could, is the one you lost," Mr. Blackwood said. "I'm sure being a postmortem medium in the pre-supernatural revolution wasn't easy. On one hand, Warren had people knocking on his door all the time, trying to get him to speak to their dead relative, friend, or whatever. Or if they needed help with exorcisms and hauntings. Then, on the other, people were scared to death of what he could do. He couldn't win."

When asked if he believed the rumors of why Warren built so many rooms, Mr. Blackwood had this to say: "It had nothing to do with children. He just wanted to keep himself busy. Some people in the community thought he killed Abigail. In reality, all of our family records indicate he loved Abigail deeply and was extremely distraught after her death. He couldn't deal with all of their accu-sations or requests, so he threw himself into a different kind of work, hoping it would alleviate his pain. Together, they only had one son, William. So, building and remodeling became something they were able to do together as William got older. Then, it turned into an obsession that was passed down from generation to genera-tion. My father was the same, until he passed the house on to me a couple of years ago. We've each added our own special touch to the house, continuing Warren's legacy and adding our own personal mark."

Mr. Blackwood was more than gracious, granting a tour around the sprawling estate. He pointed out various features of the home, including the additions he, himself, has made to the manor. They include transforming what used to be Abigail's parlor into a bedroom for his young daughter.

"She loves the view out into the courtyard and I just can't seem to say no to her," he laughed.

Other interesting aspects of the home include the expansive courtyard and view of his large pond. However, it was clear the home is where his heart is. Mr. Blackwood hinted a number of times that the home has many hidden realms to it that he hopes to one day show his daughter.

He also described the house as having a mind of its own at times. Or, perhaps better stated, "more residents" than you'd expect. Over the centuries, it has seen many people come and go. However, not all who entered the residence left, according to Mr. Blackwood.

"There are definitely ghosts wandering these halls. I feel them from time to time, but unfortunately, I'm unable to see them. I can only vaguely sense them. I wonder about my daughter at times, but she's still too young to be sure what—if any—powers she may possess. Regardless, I still do my part, making sure the community is safe from harmful or unwanted unearthly energies. The cata-

combs on the grounds act as a final resting place for many of the early supernaturals, who were scared of persecution after their death. They needed assurances their remains wouldn't be desecrated. My family has been entrusted to that task ever since."

When pressed further about this, Mr. Blackwood declined, stating, "Blackwood Manor has many secrets. It has to maintain a few of them."

My eyes widen and I read the last few sentences again.

Catacombs?

Since when do we have catacombs on the property? And where in the hell are they?

CHAPTER 10
WHO'S OUT THERE?

I f there's one thing I've learned about my house, it's that its secrets unfold in their own time. If Abigail wanted to direct me to the catacombs, she could have easily told me about it. Instead, she wanted me to find this information on my own.

Why?

I pull up to the front of the house, parking Blue as close to the door as possible, and hop out. Once I walk around to the other side, I grab my backpack and close the door. As I turn to the manor, I scan the outside of the enormous building with more than a little suspicion, and maybe a blossoming sense of awe. I've lived here for nearly six months and it's still a mystery to me. Part of me wonders if I'll ever understand its whole history.

Straightening my shoulders, I inhale a crisp January breath and head inside. The midafternoon sun is hanging heavy in the sky, blaring through the barren tree branches and into the windows. It won't be long before the sun sets completely, so I need to hurry.

"Dad? Dad, are you home?" I call out, hoping to have a word and pin him down on the information I found today. If anyone knows where the catacombs are—it's going to be him.

When silence greets me, I drop my backpack on the hall tree bench and make my way to the large dining room, hoping to find him in there. Instead, the enormous table is pristine. With all the time I've been spending at Wade's new apartment, I've hardly had any time to catch up with him to see how he's doing.

Guilt twists through my insides and I recoil from the idea of hunting him down about this before I make a point to see how he's doing. In fact, I really should make it more of a point to have deliberate conversations with my parents and make them more of a priority. Even if it's just a phone call once a week or a conversation in the hall. I'd hate for either of them to think I only come to them when I need something. Even if it's sorta the truth.

I pull my cell phone out of my pocket and set a reminder to call Mom and another one to talk with Dad. At least technology should be able to pull me outta my own head once in a while. Sighing to myself, I return the phone to my pocket and walk into the kitchen.

"Ah, Ms. Autumn," says a man with peppered grey hair and a warm smile. He finishes putting some meat into the freezer and closes the door. "It's a pleasure to finally make your acquaintance. Your father has spoken very highly of you."

He wipes off his hands with the kitchen towel, then extends one. "I'm James."

I walk up, shaking his hand, and narrow my gaze.

"The housekeeper," he says, apparently sensing my confusion.

"Oh, right," I say, shaking away the cobwebs. "Sorry, it's just it's been so long since Dad told me about you. I forgot…"

"It's to be expected. I try to stay out of the way as much as possible. However, your father may be away for a bit of time and he asked that I stock the kitchen up for you," James says, reaching for one of the canvas bags of groceries on the counter and opening it.

"I appreciate that. Any idea where he's going?" I ask, leaning against the counter and crossing my arms over my chest.

It's not like I have a right to keep track of his every movement, but a little bit of warning from him would be nice. But something tells me all his years of bachelorhood are hardwired in now.

"I'm sorry, he didn't say, and it's not entirely my place to ask," James says, pulling out a package of strawberries and a bunch of bananas from the bag. He tips his chin at a notepad beside the cordless phone. "He only left me that note."

I walk over to the counter and pick up the pad. The writing is faint, like he scribbled it quickly, but still legible.

James, I'm going to be gone for a while. Look after Autumn.

"I see. Well, thank you for doing all of this. Do I—is there anything I'm supposed to do? Like tip you or something?" I ask, a little well of panic erupting in my gut.

I have absolutely no idea how this works.

James chuckles. "No, Ms. Autumn. It's all part of the job."

Relief floods my body because I don't carry a scrap of cash on me. So, unless he has an ATM hiding around the corner, the chances of giving him a tip is pretty much nil anyway.

"Okay, well, I'm gonna go get some, uh...homework done," I say, pushing myself back from the counter and heading toward the door. "It was really nice to meet you."

James tips his head cordially. "Likewise."

Shooting him a lopsided grin and a quick wave, I make a quick exit and head back out toward the main entry. Scooping up my backpack, I walk down the hallway to my bedroom with faster-than-normal steps. My mind twists and turns over possible areas to look for the catacombs. If Dad's not going to be home for a while, I'm going to have to do this on my own. Or maybe press Abigail on it, if she'll let me.

I swing open my bedroom door, dropping my backpack onto my bed, then walk over to the large windows and take a seat. My eyes scan the courtyard, trying to spot anything out of place—or something that could be an entrance to the catacombs from here.

Shaking my head, I twist around, calling out, "Abigail— are you here? I need a word with you."

I hold my breath, waiting for her specter to arrive, but after a few minutes, it's evident she doesn't plan to join me. Either deliberately or she's busy doing whatever it is ghosts do when they're gone.

My gaze falls to the floor and I can't help but wonder... what *do* ghosts do with their time?

Inhaling deeply, I stand up and pull my gloves from my jacket pockets. Tugging them on, I walk out of my bedroom and down the hallway that leads out to the back-yard. If there are catacombs somewhere on the grounds, there has to be an entrance somewhere. Who knows, maybe my abilities will guide me?

When I reach the end of the hallway, I turn right and follow it again to the very end, where the wing terminates in a little sitting area and large picture window that over-looks the edge of the pond. I honestly can't tell which area is more beautiful—my bedroom, where I can see the whole courtyard in front of the pond, or this.

The pond is frozen solid, but its location is evident by the ring of trees that arch around its circumference like they're holding it in a comforting embrace. I unlock the large wooden side door, pulling it open. The frigid breeze blazes inward, and I prop the door open with my foot so I can zip up my coat.

I take a step outside, close the door behind me, then continue a few steps into the snow-covered yard. Sweeping my eyes across the snowy landscape, there's a creeping suspicion this will not be an easy task. Not only because our yard is massive, but because the snow has covered everything in a thick blanket that makes it damn near impossible to see anything that may be on the ground.

Ignoring the voice in the back of my head telling me this is like looking for a needle in a haystack, I trudge out to the edge of the pond, hoping to get a better vantage point from its shore. After all, no one would build cata-combs too close for fear of it getting waterlogged, so it has to be somewhere on higher ground.

By the time I make it to the shore, my toes are freezing

and I curse myself for not changing into winter boots. At the water's edge, it's oddly quiet. Which is a stark departure from the bustling sounds in the fall when the geese and swans are still nearby.

Turning around to face the manor, I hold my breath, hoping to spot something to guide me. I start by looking closely at the left side of the house, the wing mostly designated to Dad—or at least, it feels that way because I never go that way unless it's to see him. I sweep my gaze to the center courtyard, but the entire space seems flat, with the exception of the landscaping and trees. However, more to the right, and the way I came, the ground does begin to slope upward.

"Who in their right mind would put catacombs here?" I say out loud, shaking my head. "The whole house is practically at the waterline."

A flash of black against the white backdrop of the snow catches my attention and I twist around to get a better look. However, as I turn, whatever it was disappears. Tugging my eyebrows in, I take a tentative step forward, trying to see if I can spot it again.

Farther along the tree line, I catch the darkness again, but this time, it looks like a hooded figure is moving away from me. Picking up speed, I rush forward trying to gain on whatever—or whoever—it is.

"Hello?" I call out, hoping my voice will make them stop. "Who's out there?"

I push my way past low brambles and mid-height branches, trying to get closer. Again, the flash of darkness moves through the trees and this time, I know it's a person. The movements and height are all too familiar.

"Cat? Is that you?" I call out.

If it is, that would be spectacular. Cat's family has been in Windhaven for nearly as long as my own. Plus, the Gilberts definitely know about some of the strange things that have gone on in my house. Maybe, just maybe, she'll know about the catacombs.

"Hey, Cat—come back, please," I call out again, hoping to get her attention so she'll stop.

Slowly, the hooded figure turns around and drops their hood.

Cat's dark hair flies wildly in the winter breeze. Remnants of her exhalation swirl around her nonexistent expression. I take a step closer and her lips press into a thin line, but she doesn't make another move.

"Cat? Is everything okay?" I say, rushing forward as I push my way past a few more branches and trees to make it to her. "What are you doing out here?"

She looks directly at me, but doesn't say anything, and it instantly puts me on guard. It reminds me of the strange vision of her I had after Wade's grandpa's funeral. I'd nearly forgotten all about that. Goosebumps flash across my skin and I pull up short, not sure I want to get any closer.

The two of us stand facing each other in a virtual stare-off, until finally, Cat's demeanor shifts.

"Autumn—I, uh... sorry. Did you say something?" she says, clearing her throat and wiping at her eyes with the back of her hand.

I take a tentative step forward and nod. "Yeah, I was just wondering if you're okay. You're on my property."

She glances over her shoulder, as if completely out of sorts. "I'm—I guess I lost track of how far I was walking."

"Is everything all right?" I say, taking another step toward her.

"Yeah, yeah...of course. I just wanted to get some fresh air," she says, her voice gruff and scratchy. Almost as if it's the first time she's used it for the day. "Wha—what about you?"

I glance around and nod, unsure how much I really want to discuss with Cat now. "Yeah, me too, I guess. It seemed like a nice afternoon to get outside for a bit. It's chilly, but not too cold."

"Yeah..." she nods, again glancing over her shoulder.

"Well, I guess I better get back. It's starting to get dark and I'm not entirely sure I want to be roaming the woods when the sun goes down. I bet it gets a lot colder," I say, jabbing a thumb over my shoulder and taking a step back. "Are you good to get home? Or..."

"I'll be fine. I know these woods like the back of my hand," she says, twisting toward her family's property.

"Okay, well...guess I'll see you tomorrow then?" I say, narrowing my gaze and trying to smile, though I'm pretty certain, if she's paying any attention to my face, it looks more like a grimace.

"Yep," she mutters, turning all the way around and trudging through the snow.

I watch her deliberate steps as she meanders away. She veers around trees and small mounds of snow, but with the way she moves, if I didn't know better, I'd think she'd been drinking.

When she's far enough away that I can barely make out her form, I turn back the way I came and start walking to my house.

Cat and I haven't been as close this semester, partly

because of the amount of time I'm spending with Wade. There's been so much crazy and he's needed some grounding to help him adjust. Just like with my parents, I should do a better job checking in and being a good friend.

God, I suck.

But Cat's been good. She's been herself and normal.

I shoot another glance over my shoulder, unable to shake away the uneasy feeling settling in my stomach.

At least, I think she has been?

Then again, what if there *is* something off about Cat— what would that mean?

A terrifying thought pops into my head and I shiver.

What if her resurrection didn't go as well as we thought?

CHAPTER 11
MAYBE IT WAS FATE

I f something isn't right with Cat, how would anyone
know for sure? Is there some sort of supernatural
test we could do to figure it out? Like a magical
blood test or scan?

Even if there was, would I be able to get her to agree
to it?

I kick at the snow mound at my feet, wishing this
gnawing feeling at the pit of my stomach would go away. I
flit my gaze to the area in the woods where I saw her
yesterday.

What if there's nothing wrong and I'm just imagining
something that isn't there? Worse yet, what if it's all me—
in *my* head?

"Hey, where are you? You seem pretty far away," Wade
says, reaching out and placing a hand on my upper arm,
then tugging me close.

I shake away my trepidation and look up at his
concerned face. With everything that's been going on, the

last thing I want to do is worry him more. "I was just thinking about the catacombs. I have no idea where the entrance could be, but I know we need to figure it out. Abigail wouldn't have led me to the information if it wasn't important to the questions I was asking."

"It's here somewhere. I'm sure we'll find it. Granted, this snow isn't making it easy..." he says, placing his hand above his eyebrows and scanning the landscape. His eyes stop briefly on the gardening sheds and boathouse. "There are so many places we could check. And it's not like your yard is tiny."

"Right? We've been out here for ages and still...*nothing*," I groan.

"What if the entrance isn't outside?" Wade offers, dropping his hand.

Shaking my head, I turn to him, "Where else would it be?"

Wade shrugs. "Have you looked in any of these outbuilding or inside the house? I mean, if I wanted to protect an important burial site, I'd make sure no one else has access to it. Look at what happened to my grandpa."

My eyes widen and I blink back surprise. "I never thought of that—or put the two together. I guess I just figured, if it's a burial site, you'd want to keep it outside."

"Did the article mention if the manor itself was on top of the catacombs?" he asks, shifting his gaze back to the house.

"No, it just said it houses the catacombs. God, I wish my dad were here. I could just ask him," I say, cursing the poor timing.

"Is it really that hard to get ahold of him? I mean, can't

you call him?" Wade asks, scratching at his chin with his pointer finger and settling his silver gaze on me. His eyes are practically the color of the snow, as his pupils narrow in the sunlight. "Doesn't he have a cellphone?"

I bite my lip and snicker. "That would mean my dad entered the 21st century. No, he's still pretty old school. Truth be told, I'm surprised the house has internet. I've never even seen him use a computer."

Wade's dark eyebrows lift. "Geez, it's like living with my grandpa."

I nod emphatically. "Very possibly."

Wade's phone dings loudly, echoing through the snow-covered trees.

"Speak of the devil and he shall text you," Wade chuckles, reaching into his back pocket and pulling out his phone. He turns it over, having a quick look at the screen. Dropping his arm, he starts to place it back into his pocket but stops and does a double take. Concern spreads across his features as he holds it out again and unlocks it. With each passing moment, his eyebrows knit themselves closer.

"What is it?" I ask, unable to help myself.

Wade's jaw clenches and unclenches. "Looks like news about what happened in Mistwood Point cemetery has made it to the rumor mill. Someone thinks they found what's left of the decomposing bodies. And of course, the tipped-over tombstone is getting people riled up all over again. There's a newspaper article on it."

"Did someone send that to you?" I ask, surprised.

"Nah, I have a Google alert set up. I figured it was just a matter of time. Ugh, I really wish this shit wasn't happening. I'm sure it'll somehow make its way back to me," he mutters, closing his eyes and returning the phone to his pocket.

"You don't know that," I say, placing a hand on his arm, trying to reassure him.

Glancing down at where my hand rests, he places his over the top. "I appreciate what you're saying, but I wasn't even in town when my grandpa's columbarium was destroyed. They still found a way to make it my fault. We were actually *there* for this one. Shit, if they find out you were with..." His face loses some of its color and his nostrils widen.

"Don't worry about me. I can handle myself, Wade. Besides, we're in this together. We will get it all sorted out," I say, refusing to let uncertainty or fear get the better of me.

"I wish I had your positivity. I really do, but I don't know... Things have a way of going pear-shaped around me." He frowns.

"Good thing I like pears," I say, shooting him a cheesy grin.

He flashes me a smile, but it does't quite reach his eyes.

"Oh, come on. Please don't crack up on me now. *I'm* supposed to be Drusilla, not you," I say, sticking out my tongue.

Wade sighs. "According to the article, they're bringing in some federal supernatural investigators and something about a world-renowned psychic who deals with these types of unusual cases."

"Good. If they're so famous, they should be able to sort all of this out. Right?"

He groans, covering his face with both hands. "We were there, remember? I had to kill both of them...*again*."

"But that wasn't your fault. They were attacking—"

"And how long do you think it will take for people to accept that one? Even if they're pointed directly at it, most people can't see the truth for themselves. They're more than willing to keep living in their made-up worlds because it's easier than saying they were wrong. People have already made their minds up about me. Maybe coming to the school was a bad idea..." he says, running his hand through his hair and taking a few steps away.

"I'm sure it's not that bad. The psychic could figure out who's *actually* summoning the revenants. Wouldn't that be a good thing?" I ask as I follow him. "We could use an ally at this point."

Wade covers his face with both hands, sighing into them. After a moment, he peeks through his fingers. "You really have far too much faith in others. You know that?"

I press my lips into a thin line.

Wade chuckles, dropping his hands from his face and placing them alongside mine. "I love that about you. I really do. I wish I had that—but my life experience has taught me something vastly different. Despite my cool, calm demeanor, I'm a cluster of raw nerves most days."

"I'm sorry," I mutter. Wrapping my arms around him, I close my eyes, wishing all of this craziness was behind us and we could just relax for once. I don't remember the last time we were able to spend some time together as a normal couple.

As if sensing my frustration, Wade says, "Hey, how about we get out of here? Forget all this graveyard and catacomb shit and just...*be*? I need some Autumn time."

I lift my head, my lips sliding into an easy smile. "It's like you're in my brain."

"Well, we are soul mates," he says, lifting his hand to my jaw and sliding his thumb across my bottom lip.

I inhale sharply, my heart tripping over itself. Until this very moment, I hadn't realized how disjointed and almost disconnected I've been feeling, but with those simple words, everything seems brighter. "Soul mates? You really think so?"

The corners of his eyes crease, and the sparkle in their depths is back. "Of course. How else do you explain the way we found each other? It was *fate*."

My mind drifts to the evening we first met. His easy-going nature and natural charisma... Both of us in the graveyard, sharing so many of the same loves in pop culture. Both supernatural in our own ways.

Maybe he's right. *Maybe it was fate.*

Wade grins, leaning forward and brushing his lips to mine.

The spark that follows ignites immediately and I sigh into him, wishing we could just let the entire world and all of its crazy fade away forever.

The chill air whips around us, blowing my hair around us like a shroud of protection. As his lips burn down on mine, his kiss warms every nerve ending of my body, melting away any doubts and worries. Instead, it's all replaced with the desire to be totally his. Body and soul.

Wade pulls back, his eyes half-open with the same dreamy daze. After a moment, he shudders and says, "Let's get inside and see what kind of mischief we can find ourselves in."

I quirk an eyebrow, but my lips slide into a smirk. "Well, we do have the entire manor all to ourselves…"

He tips his head and returns my expression. "That we certainly do."

Reaching out, I slide my hand in his and lead the way through the trees and back toward the manor. I could kick myself for having walked as far away as we have. Instead, I pick up speed.

Laughing out loud, Wade pulls my hand back, twirling me around in the snow. He steps forward and instinctively, I take a step back, placing my back against one of the large oak trees. Without a word, he bends forward, pressing his body against mine. Placing his hands on either side of my shoulders, he watches me intensely. In response, I arch my back, pressing my hips forward. I slide my hands around his waist and rest them on the small of his back.

He groans, bending again to press his lips to mine. There's more force behind this kiss, as he flicks my upper lip with the tip of his tongue. He raises his hands to entwine his fingers in my hair. I open my mouth, unable to stop the moan that escapes, and he takes the opportunity to explore further. His tongue teases my own in a dance of mastery all his own—he knows exactly what to do to make my body temperature rise.

I slide my hands farther, planting them firmly on his butt, as I pull his hips to mine, grinding forward. This time, Wade practically growls, lurching forward and pressing his lips to my neck. His hot breath sends waves of goosebumps surging through my body, making me shudder.

"God, I want you, Autumn…" he whispers against my skin, trying to calm his breath.

I swallow hard, trying to think through this heady aura of desire. Biting my lip, I tip my head to the manor. "Come on, let's get inside."

His dark eyelashes flutter and nostrils flare as he pulls in a deep breath. Nodding to himself, he takes a tentative step back, holding out his hand for me. As I take it, he pulls me upright. Shooting him a sideways smile, another shudder rolls through my body. After the months of craziness, the moment finally feels right.

Nervous energy and excitement build in every cell in my body and I just want to get inside as quickly as possible. Neither of us say another word; we just make our way, listening to the quick crunching of our footsteps in the snow. With each passing step, I try to hold onto as much of the moment as possible. I don't think Wade knows just how incredibly sexy he is.

When we reach the boathouse, I pause, needing to refill my reserves. I turn to him and run my right hand through his dark locks. I'm mesmerized by the way the sunlight sparkles through the strands, highlighting the random reds and golds in his black hair.

Standing up on my toes, I pull him closer. I press my lips to his and inhale his scent of sandalwood and soap as it blends with the winter wind. I don't know what it is about his touch, or his kisses...but I could stay submerged in the feelings and sensations they evoke forever, if he'd let me.

Chuckling under his breath, he pulls back. "Come on, Autumn. It'll be much more fun inside. I promise you—"

Suddenly, Wade's eyes widen and his jaw slacks open. Within a split-second, all color drains from his face.

Pulling back, I twist around, following his tormented stare.

Less than ten feet away, I catch the tail end of an old man materializing like a dust-devil has just brought him into being. Everything about him looks as though it's made of ash and yet, somehow, still solid. As the man takes an awkward first step forward, I clasp my hands over my mouth.

It's Wade's dead grandfather.

CHAPTER 12
BUZZKILL

Instinctively, Wade springs into action, pulling me back and stepping out in front, effectively putting himself between me and his grandfather.

"Is this—normal?" I sputter, unable to take my eyes off the crumbling version of the man I barely knew.

Wade shoots me a WTF look and shakes his head. "What in the hell could *possibly* be normal about this?" He jabs his right hand, palm side up, toward his grandfather.

"I—I don't know. You said your family's powers are dormant. Maybe they don't kick in until you die?" I sputter, unable to think of anything else that makes sense.

With wide eyes, Wade turns back to his grandpa. "No, this is something else—something unnatural. I've never seen anything like this. I...have no idea what to do here."

My mind wheels through various scenarios, but none of them are good.

"Grandpa—it's me, Wade. Do you remember me?" he says, splaying his arms out wide, trying to get his grandpa's attention.

Unfortunately, there's no recognition hidden in the ashen face of the man standing before us. If anything, he looks almost feral as he crouches down, pulling his elbows back like he's about to pounce.

"Oh my god, he's another revenant," I say, tugging at Wade's arm.

"Well, yeah, I kinda figured," Wade replies, tilting his head to the side.

My heartbeat thumps loudly in my chest, and I'm acutely aware of the fact that we're highly exposed. "He shouldn't be here. We need to find a way to release him," I sputter.

Wade takes a step backward, forcing me to do the same. "Well, if you have any ideas, I'm all ears 'cause I got nothin'. This is so far outside the realm of normal for me."

"We'll have to destroy his body, just like the other ones."

"I can't kill him," Wade practically squeaks.

"Wade, he's already dead," I say, unable to even blink away.

With that, the creature lunges forward, hissing as it leaps a good five feet or more into the air. In microseconds, the ashen figure of Wade's grandpa is on top of us, stretching out its hands as it tries to grab hold of the front of Wade's leather jacket. Caught off guard by the insanely sudden movement, I jump back, slipping on an icy patch and landing hard on my backside. Wade's footing also falters, but the creature manages to intertwine its fingers with Wade's collar, taking them both down as well.

As I scramble back and away, Wade manages to kick the revenant off of him, but only for seconds before it gets its bearings and attacks again.

"Can you get that door open?" Wade yells, pressing his arms straight out and holding the creature. It snaps and snarls, trying to get at its prey as it thrusts its fingers across Wade's face.

Without even answering, I scramble to my feet and make my way to the side door of the boathouse. Clutching the handle, I give it a twist and thrust my shoulder into it, trying to get it to swing open. The resounding thud reverberates, but the door itself doesn't budge.

"Dammit," I curse, immediately scanning the area for a key. "It's locked."

I shove my hand into the potted evergreen beside the doorway but come up empty-handed.

"Just kick it in," Wade yells back, wrestling the revenant from side to side as he struggles to get himself free.

Standing on my tiptoes, I feel around the edge of the trim work. My fingertips graze the edge of something metallic as it drops into the snow beside the door. Immediately I drop to my knees, ignoring the trembling in my hands as I dig through the snow for the key. Finally, my fingertips find the cold metal and I pluck it from the snowbank. Racing to the handle, I thrust in the key and mutter a prayer under my breath that it works.

The locks groans, but clicks, and I fling the door back. "Got it."

Spinning around, I run up to the revenant, planting my foot along its side with as much force as I can muster. Luckily, the blow is enough to knock him off of Wade, at least momentarily. Thrusting my hand down, I pull Wade to his feet. The revenant turns around, makes another swipe for him, and barely misses.

"Christ, this thing won't quit," Wade huffs, his eyes wide and face flushed.

Twisting around, he grabs hold of the revenant instead, bending his legs and rushing the two of them forward into the boathouse. When he's cleared the doorway, Wade drops the odd, dusty fabric of the creature, letting momentum carry it farther into the space. Without a second's hesitation, Wade pivots, grabbing the handle and slamming the door shut.

He stands here, his hands gripping the door handle as if his life depends on it—and it does. The creature screams, howling and groping at the door on the other side.

"Here, let me lock it," I say, stepping forward and twisting the key into place.

As the lock clicks, Wade exhales loudly but doesn't remove his hands. "Do you think it knows how to unlock doors?" he whispers.

I shake my head, ignoring the fact that my entire body is trembling. "I—I don't know."

The shrieking stops on the other side and an eerie silence greets us. It's almost as if the creature has vanished completely.

"Let's not stick around to find out," Wade says, dropping the door handle and grabbing my hand.

Together, we race for the house, putting as much distance between us and the boathouse as possible. The moment we get to the door of the manor, we open it and dart inside. Without a second thought, we both turn around, thrusting our arms out and slamming the door shut. With Wade still pressing it closed, I flip the lock on the handle and set the deadbolt.

Removing his hands, Wade takes a step back, pressing his hands to his mouth. "Holy shit. That was—"

"Scary?" I breathe, slumping to my knees.

"Intense," Wade says, nodding and sliding to the floor with his back against the door.

"What the hell was that all about? I mean, was that really him? Or?" I clutch at my chest, trying to take a deep, cleansing breath and failing miserably.

Wade shakes his head, his own breathing jagged. "No clue. Sure as hell looked like him, though."

"So, what do we do now? I mean, he can't stay in the boathouse forever..."

Wade shudders. "Who knows if he's still in there *now*. Did you see the way he materialized? It was like his ashes were somehow melded together and reanimated."

"Yeah, that was crazy. But if you really want to know whether or not he's still in there, we can go back out and..."

"Nope, nope..." Wade says, shaking his head. "I'm good with assuming he's trapped. At least until we figure out what to do next."

I bite my lip, thinking through possible scenarios. "What if we call the authorities?"

"And told them what? Hey, guys, there's a dead guy trapped in the boathouse and we could use some help. Granted, he was recently turned to ash, but he's now running around like a spry chicken. Wanna come and check it out?"

"They have people who can handle this. They have to, right? So, what if we just told them we have a revenant locked in the boathouse? We don't have to say who we think it is. Do we?"

Wade considers for a few seconds. "I'm pretty sure it's part of their job to figure it out. Then all that stuff I was just talking about gets even worse. Not only were we at the Mistwood Point cemetery when the others attacked—now this. Royally screwed comes to mind."

"Why are they targeting us?" I ask, wishing there was an easy answer.

Wade shrugs. "God, I wish I knew."

I sigh, shifting around to sit beside him. Tipping my head back to rest against the door, I lean into him and place my hand on his thigh. The beautiful, sexy moment between us has passed, but an absurd giggle escapes my lips.

I shoot Wade a sideways glance and stifle another laugh. "Well, nothing like being chased by a dead grandpa to kill the mood."

He snickers, shifting himself forward into a crouching position, then stands up. "Right? We just can't catch a break." Wade extends his arm, offering a hand and helping me up. "Come on, let's see if we can find any magical rules about revenants."

"Like what kind?"

"Like, if they materialize out of ashes, do they keep their form once they've corporealized...or not?" he says, screwing up his face.

"Good point," I say, taking off down the hallway. "Do you want to go back to the school? Or do you want to do it from here? There could be something in my Postmortem Communication classwork, or maybe even Advanced Life Energies."

We turn the corner, heading back to my bedroom. Wade keeps his eyes trained on each window as we go past, as if he's expecting the revenant to come bursting through at any moment.

"At this point, I don't know," he finally says. "If we do any research from here outside your lessons, we have a digital trail back to us. If we go to the school, there's still a good chance it will come back to us if the feds search their databases for anything specific. We have to log in with our student IDs."

"What if I try to summon Abigail again? Maybe if I can get her—"

Wade shakes his head. "I don't think she's willing to dish out information when I'm around. But I guess you can try."

I stop walking to grab hold of his wrist. "What makes you say that?"

Wade narrows his gaze and bites his lower lip. "Just a feeling I get. She really only comes to you when I'm not around," he says, shrugging. "But I could be wrong."

There's more to his hunch than he's letting on. I can see it in his face. But I think back, trying to figure out if she's ever been active when Wade's been around. Nothing comes to me—at least, not where she's been helpful. "Hmmm, you might be right."

Wade shrugs and starts walking down the hall again. I follow quietly after, my mind whirling with the recent events. The revenant, the attack, everything Wade's said about being suspected of this. Plus, this thing with Abigail. If it's true, why would it be? She was with me, helping me to bring Cat back. But other than that, she's never really been active unless I'm alone.

Stepping out in front, Wade opens the door to my bedroom, then moves back. "After you."

I shoot him a wary smile, walking into my bedroom and heading over to my desk. "So what do you want to do? Look in my lessons first? Or do a search?"

Again, Wade's phone sounds, but this time it's like the Tardis has landed as his ringtone blares out. He shoots me a confused look, pulling his phone from his pocket and wiping it across his pant leg.

"Dammit, the screen's cracked," he mutters. "Guess that'll teach me to leave it in my back pocket."

"Yeah, because you never know when the undead will chase you around," I nod, shooting him a sideways glance as I flip open my laptop.

"Shit," Wade curses under his breath.

I spin around on my chair and quirk an eyebrow. "What now?"

He takes a seat on the edge of my bed. Gripping the phone tightly in his left hand, he shakes his head. Without a word, he holds his arm out and passes his phone to me.

Confused, I take it from him and look down. Playing on the screen is a close-up shot of Wade at the Mistwood Point cemetery—just as he pushed over the tombstone. I flinch as it lands on the revenant.

Beneath the video is an anonymous text message:

I know this sort of thing runs in your family. You don't belong here. Get out of Windhaven and never come back. You've got until the end of the week or this video goes viral.

CHAPTER 13

PROVE IT

"What in the hell?" I spit, unable to think of anything beyond the rage coursing through my body. I swear, I'm getting emotional whiplash just in the last half hour. "Who would do something like this? And *why?*"

"My sentiments exactly," Wade says, standing up and running his hands through his dark locks. "See? What did I tell you? I knew shit was gonna hit the fan. It always does."

"What do you think this has got to do with your family?" I say, handing Wade back his phone.

Wade shakes his head and raises his palms to the ceiling. "How in the hell do I know? Maybe they know about my dad being a suspect the last time this sort of thing happened? Or maybe they just think I'm not good enough to go to Windhaven Academy. I guess they'd be right..."

"Does this have anything to do with what Dominic said last semester?" I ask, my mind wheeling through a tornado of thoughts.

Wade drops his hands and his eyebrows turn up in the middle. "Dominic?"

"You know, the guy who keyed my car? When we were at the Bourbon Room he said something about how you shouldn't be here, too..." My eyes widen and I cover my mouth. "Oh, God. You don't think it's him, do you?"

"Well, if it is, he's gonna wish he'd chosen a different pastime," Wade says, clenching his fists.

Standing up, I close my laptop. "Guess it's a good thing I still have my coat on. Come on, let's go."

Bewilderment flashes through Wade's features. "Go? Go where?"

"We're going to resolve this right now. We're going to Dominic's."

I don't wait for a response. Instead, I walk straight out the door and down the hallway. If Dominic is a part of this, so help me, *I'll* hurt him. I just don't understand why he'd have it in for Wade. Or why he'd want him out of town. None of this is making any sense. But one thing's for sure—if it's him, we're going to get it out of him and tell him where to shove it.

Wade follows on my heels, but picks up speed so he can walk beside me. "What exactly are we going to say to him? Shouldn't we think this through a little bit before we go marching over there?"

"No, I think we need to nail him down before he has any time to come up with excuses or alibis," I say, shooting Wade a sideways glance as I fling open the front door.

Wade grabs hold of my right wrist, spinning me around to face him. "We need to be careful. What is this Dominic guy capable of? What powers does he have? I mean, he said something about being able to hear my thoughts that day—"

"Yeah, he's a psychic," I say, pressing my lips into a thin line. Suddenly, the idea doesn't seem like the best of choices. What if he can read what happened between me and Colton last semester? Would he be willing to spill it if he picks up on it?

"Okay, is that all?" Wade says, narrowing his eyes.

I blink away the thoughts and shrug. "I think so? Honestly, I don't really know a lot about him. I don't overly pay attention to what other people are doing. I'm so wrapped up in my own chaos, you know?"

Wade sighs, running his hand over his lips. "Okay, that's okay. At least that helps me to understand where he might be coming from."

"Good, then let's do this," I say, leaning forward and giving him a kiss on his cheek. "We'll get this sorted out."

"Yeah, okay. But remember, we gotta be careful. If the revenant escaped—"

I bound down the front steps before he has time to finish his sentence, racing over to Blue. I can't live my life in fear, locked away in the manor. But at the same time, I'm not about to linger out in the open, either. Just in case.

Without another word, Wade gets into the passenger seat and buckles in. When I put the vehicle into drive, the wheels spin on the slushy driveway as I pull around the loop faster than I probably should. Wade doesn't say a word, though. Instead, he sits with his arms crossed over his body and his eyebrows practically creating a crater on his forehead. Both of us eye the sides of the road as if something could jump out at any moment.

"It's not far. He just lives down the road," I say, cutting through the thick silence.

"Good. I don't know how much suspense I can handle in one day," Wade whispers.

I reach out, tugging at his sleeve, hoping he'll release his hand from his arm. He turns to look at me and I hold my hand out, trying to shoot him a sincere smile. "Everything will be okay. You're not going anywhere. I refuse to let you."

Wade snickers, but reaches for my hand, sliding his palm against mine. "Yeah, well, at this point, I don't know that it's up to us. I mean, hell, it's like the entire universe really doesn't want me here."

"Well, that's a bit dramatic," I say, snickering under my breath.

Wade glances down to his knees and says sarcastically, "But is it though?" Turning his head, he looks out the window.

"Is there something you're not telling me?" I ask. "Is there anyone else that doesn't want you here?"

Taking a deep breath, Wade bites down on the side of his cheek.

"Wade?" I press.

"I don't know. Maybe?" he finally says.

My eyes widen as I flip the turn signal to turn down Dominic's drive. "Maybe? You don't know?"

"No, I don't. I mean, I don't think they'd have enough pull to do something like this."

"Who?" I say, putting the vehicle into park in front of Dominic's large, white manor.

Wade's tongue skirts across his lower lips and he tips his head to the house. "Let's check this first. Like you said, we don't want to eliminate the element of surprise. Come on."

This time, it's Wade who makes a quick exit, leaving me scrambling after him.

Before we even make it to the door, Dominic steps outside. His white-blond hair and outfit are disheveled, like he just crawled out of bed.

"Dominic, we—" I begin, but he raises a hand, cutting me off.

"Autumn, between the two of you, there is no need to even open your mouth. God, I could hear you coming a mile away. Literally," he says, taking a deep breath and rolling his eyes.

"I'm sorry, are we interrupting your *sleep* time?" Wade says, his jaw hardening as he steps into Dominic's space.

Dom's light eyebrow arches high. He presses all five fingertips in his right hand against Wade's chest, gently pushing him back a step. "Actually, you're just lucky I put clothes back on. I was a bit..." he looks over his shoulder, "*preoccupied*. Maybe you should try it. Might take this *edge* off."

"Stop playing games with us. If you can hear our thoughts, you know why we're here. What do you know?" Wade growls, his silver eyes darkening as his eyebrows press down.

"All I'm saying is you need to get laid."

Wade steps forward, grabbing Dominic by the front of his shirt, lifting him up to his tiptoes. "Answer the goddamn question."

Dominic clutches at Wade's hands as he struggles to maintain his own balance.

"Wade," I warn, placing my hands on his left arm.

Refusing to look at me, the lines on his jaw harden, but he lets Dom drop back to his own footing.

"It wasn't me. Whatever it is that's got your tidy whities in a twist, it wasn't me. Like I said, I was a bit busy with *Natasha*," he says, shifting his gaze from Wade to me and back again.

"Prove it," Wade says, his expression hardening. He releases his grip on Dominic's shirt, thrusting him back a bit.

"How? Bring her out here in her birthday suit? I'm sure that'll go down well with—" he points a finger my direction.

"Don't care. Prove to me you're not a lying weasel," Wade says through clenched teeth. "My life is on the line here and I don't take it lightly."

Dominic rolls his eyes and sighs. "So dramatic."

Wade reaches out for Dominic, who sidesteps his clutches.

"Fine, fine," Dom says, straightening his shirt and glancing my direction. His gaze turns from a passing look to one of concentration. After a moment his eyebrows tighten and his jaw slacks open. "You have a *what* in your boathouse?"

"It's not a what," Wade says. "It's a who. Now, get the girl."

"God, all right. Come on," Dominic says, shooting me another surprised look before opening the door and letting us inside. "She's not going to like this."

"I couldn't honestly care less," Wade says, his voice low.

Dominic leads us through a large entryway by the standard of any normal house, but it's still about half the size of the one at my house. The inside isn't at all what I expected. Rather than being immaculate, like the way he typically dresses for school, there are aspects of the home that look like they need some extensive work done. While the house is spacious and has some beautiful elements to the internal architecture, like intricate crown molding and woodwork, it's as though its been left to its own devices for far too long. Parts of the plaster on the walls is discoloring or flaking off, especially in the high parts of the ceilings.

Dominic shoots me a sideways glance and I swear his face flushes. But he remains silent as he walks up the large flight of stairs to the right, and takes a quick turn, following the upper landing around to the left.

"Hey, babe—it's me. Can you make sure you're covered up?" Dominic says, peering through the doorway as he opens it a crack.

There's a shuffle inside, but a woman's voice filters out into the hallway. "What's going on, Dom? Everything okay?"

Dominic nods his head, opening the door enough so we can see inside. "Yeah, I just gotta—"

Wade steps forward, pushing his way past Dominic. Surprised by his forcefulness, I follow after him, stopping just inside the door. A blond girl I've never seen before sits in the middle of a large four-poster bed, clutching red satin sheets to her chest. Her eyes are the size of big blue pools as she looks from us back to Dominic.

"Satisfied?" Dominic hisses, stepping back out into the hallway and flagging us to come out.

Wade shoots an apologetic glance at the woman, "S-sorry to bother you." He diverts his eyes and walks out the way he came.

I turn to the woman and wave awkwardly. "Sorry for the interruption."

She blinks wildly but doesn't say a word.

Following after both of the guys, I make sure to close the door on my way out.

"Well, that was an experience," I say, lifting my eyebrows and crossing my arms.

"Now, if you don't mind, I'd love for the two of you to get the hell out of my house," Dominic says, stepping aside and pointing at the stairs.

Wade hangs his head in defeat, but only gets a few steps before he turns back to Dominic. "If it's not you, then who the hell is doing this? You're psychic, right? Can you help us?"

"My abilities don't work like that, man. It's not a magic trick, for fucksake. Ask Autumn. I don't always get all the information," Dominic says, jabbing a thumb my direction.

Wade looks my direction, but I hold both hands up. "Don't bring me into this. I barely know how *my* powers work."

"Can you try?" Wade pleads. "Someone is raising the dead and now they're threatening me."

"Look, I'll see what I can do. But not now," Dominic says, placing a hand on his door handle. "I have company."

"I don't have much time," Wade begins.

Dominic opens the door to his bedroom and takes a step inside. "Kinda not my problem." Without another word, he closes the door.

"Dammit," Wade curses under his breath, glancing in

my direction. "Sorry about all of this, Autumn. After what you said, I was so sure…"

I shake my head, reaching for his hand. "No, it's my fault. I'm the one who brought up Dominic. Come on, let's get out of here. We need to come up with another plan."

Wade's lips press into a thin line and he nods.

Without another word, I walk for the stairs, refusing to let go of Wade's hand. Together we exit Dominic's house, stepping down the icy steps and onto the driveway. The driveway, I now notice, has barely been snowplowed. Wade hops into the passenger seat and slams the door.

Lowering my head in defeat, I walk around to the driver's side. When I reach the door, I glance back at Dominic's house.

If it's not him, then who?

Sighing to myself, I open the driver's side door and slide inside. "So, what next? What do we do?" I say, closing the door and turning to face him. I'm a bundle of raw nerves, so I can't even fathom how he must be feeling right now.

Wade's jaw clenches and he shrugs. "What can I do? I have a dead grandpa trapped in your boathouse that I need to do something with pretty damn fast. And now, someone wants me to leave or he'll basically end me. I'm pretty much stuck between a rock and a fucking mountain."

CHAPTER 14
CONFESSIONS

I f we can't figure out who sent the text to Wade, does that mean he'll leave Windhaven behind? Could he really do that, even if he's innocent?

Taking a deep breath, I can't help but wish my own powers were tied more to telepathy and not necromancy or talking to the dead. At least then, maybe I could do some good. Instead, I feel so useless.

"Autumn, before we head back to your place, I think we need to go to the police," Wade finally says, cutting through the pregnant silence.

My gaze snaps over to him. "Are you serious?"

"What other choice do I have?" he says, clenching his jaw. "If I don't go to the police with what I do know...and that video goes out, it'll be too late. It'll be framed however this asshat wants to frame it. Then, nothing will matter. The police—or anyone else, for that matter—won't believe a word I have to say. My only chance is to turn over what I know before it bites me in the ass."

My lips snap shut and a stab of guilt sweeps through

me. His words bring me right back to my own inner dilemma with what happened with Colton. He's a hell of a lot braver than I am, that's for sure.

"All right," I say, driving past the turn to Blackwood Manor and heading into town. "I hope you know what you're doing."

Wade inhales sharply, reaching for my hand. "So do I."

We drive the next few minutes in silence; neither one of us wanting to convince the other of a different plan. As much as I hate to admit it, this feels right. If Wade can get to the police first, telling them what he knows, he stands a chance. Maybe we could completely disarm the situation.

As we reach the edge of town, my back begins to tighten and I find myself sitting up straighter in the seat. "So, we're almost there. Have you thought about what you want to say?"

Wade nods. "It's all I've been doing since we left."

"Good. What do you want me to do?" I say, turning down Main Street and heading to the town square.

"Nothing. Let me do all the talking. Okay?" he says, running his hand over his mouth. "I don't want to pull you into this at all, if I can help it. Deal?"

"But—"

"Promise me," Wade says, cutting me off. His eyes plead with mine.

I nod. "Okay."

My pulse quickens as I pull up to the police station, parking in one of the diagonal spaces right outside the front entrance. The visitor parking is practically vacant, but there are six police cars lined up around the corner. For such a small town, it seems a little like overkill at the precinct.

"Wonder why there are so many cop cars," I mutter, putting Blue into park.

Wade's eyebrows tug inward as his gaze sweeps over them. "Let's hope the fact that they're here is good news. It means there isn't reason to be out and about."

I nod, kicking open my door. "Good point."

Opening his own door, Wade follows me. When we reach the sidewalk, he steps out in front, making sure he's first to the door. He pulls it back, allowing me to head inside first. As soon as the door closes, he takes the lead again, walking up to the glass-enclosed front desk.

A woman with dark skin and big brown eyes looks up. She's barely older than we are, but she holds her shoulders back in an air of authority as we both approach. Her name badge reads "Thompson."

"May I help you?" Officer Thompson asks, her voice soft and almost musical.

Wade swallows hard, tipping his chin. "Yeah, uh—is Sheriff Gordon here, by chance?"

"He is. Can I tell him who's asking?" she says, her dark eyebrows barely moving.

Clearing his throat, Wade reaches for my hand and says, "Wade. Wade Hoffman. I'm a friend of his cousin, Chelsea Gordon."

Recognition flashes through the officer's eyes and she nods. "Okay, Mr. Hoffman, have a seat. Sheriff Gordon will come get you."

"Thanks," Wade says, twisting around and eyeing the seating.

There are two sections, each with four chairs that have been clamped together. There are no tables or magazines to preoccupy those who take a seat. Instead, they all just face each other in a sort of seated standoff.

"I forgot about Sheriff Gordon being related to your landlord. That was a good call," I say, leaning in and whispering in Wade's ear.

Wade feigns a smile. "Yeah, I figured if nothing else, I'd have a little bit of leverage by talking to him. At least Chelsea knows me. You know?"

My insides clench and I try to suppress the irrational welling of jealousy springing up from her name. She's been nothing but nice, but I can't help but feel a little pang of possessiveness.

"Mr. Hoffman?" a man says, extending a hand as he enters the lobby. He has the same ginger hair and green eyes as his cousin and it's easy to see the family resemblance.

Wade immediately stands up. "Yes, hi."

"What can I help you with?" Sheriff Gordon says. His eyes crease at their edges, immediately disarming any apprehension lingering in me. Another trait he shares with his cousin.

"I—uh," Wade begins. "Is there anywhere we could talk privately?"

Sheriff Gordon quirks an eyebrow. His lips tug downward as he nods. "Sure, follow me." He turns on his heel, flashes a badge that opens the door he came through, and holds it open so we can follow behind him.

Wade reaches for my hand, and together we follow after the sheriff to a small conference room down the hall. Sheriff Gordon steps inside, standing beside the door until we both walk in and take a seat at the small table. Without a word, he quietly clicks it shut and sits down opposite us.

Again, he flashes a grin and extends his hand to me. "I'm sorry, I don't think I caught your name."

"Autumn Blackwood," I say, shaking his hand.

"Ah, yes," he nods. "Lyle's girl. I thought you looked familiar. Been awhile. Are you back in town now?"

I narrow my gaze, trying to process. "I—yes, actually. I'm going to school at Windhaven Academy."

His eyebrows rise into his hairline, but he nods absently. "Certain amount of sense to that."

I press my lips together and tap the top of the table with my fingertips.

"So," Sheriff Gordon says, turning back to Wade, "What can I do for you?"

Wade's nostrils flare as he breathes in deeply. "I have a confession to make."

The sheriff's eyes widen, and his jaw hardens. He looks over his shoulder at the mirror behind him and pulls his chair in tighter to the table. "Before we go much further, do you mind if I record this?" he says, pulling out a small voice recorder from his breast pocket and placing it on the table between them.

Wade doesn't say anything, but he shakes his head.

Sheriff Gordon tips his head. "All right, what kind of confession are we talking here?"

Clasping his hands together, Wade drops his gaze to his fingers. An awkward pause follows, and he licks his lower lip. "I know what happened at Mistwood Point Cemetery last week. I know I should have come forward sooner. It's just—"

"Okay, hold up," Sheriff Gordon says, holding a hand out. "Are you saying you were there?"

"Yeah, I was there," Wade says, refusing to look my direction.

The desire to speak up and say I was, too, almost bowls me over. Wade must sense it, because he taps his foot against mine. Clamping my lips shut, I focus on watching the two men's reactions.

"All right, go on," the sheriff says.

"The cemetery director called and let me know my grandfather's columbarium was fixed, so I went to have a look. I wanted to make sure things were restored to the way they were before," Wade says, swallowing hard. "Especially since his ashes haven't been..."

The sheriff holds very still, watching every movement Wade makes like he's waiting for something that will tell him whether or not to pounce.

"When I was there," Wade continues, his tongue skating across his lower lip as he shoots me a quick sideways glance, "I was attacked."

This was clearly not the confession the sheriff was expecting, as his eyebrows arch high. "You were attacked? Why didn't you report anything?"

Wade scratches at the back of his head. "I was afraid. I knew how things looked, and people at Windhaven Academy were already assuming I was involved with the desecration earlier because one of the graves that was vandalized was my grandfather's. I didn't want to draw any more attention to myself if I could help it."

The sheriff's eyes narrow, but he nods. "All right, continue. Who attacked you?"

Wade casts a super-fast glance in my direction and says, "The *dead* did."

Sheriff Gordon's green eyes flash. "Excuse me?"

"The graves that were robbed—I don't think it's a prank. I think someone is raising the dead," Wade reiterates.

"Is that a thing now?" Sheriff Gordon says, scratching at his chin. "Zombies?"

"Revenants, actually," I say, unable to help myself.

The sheriff's gaze flits to me. "I've been around a long time and I've seen some weird things in this town thanks to the supers...but zombies? Now, that's new."

"Revenants," I repeat.

"Right, revenants," he nods. "Well, see, here's the thing. We've had another five or so graves desecrated over the course of the past week. I haven't checked in with the Mistwood PD, but I'll wager they'd be real interested to hear your story, Mr. Hoffman."

Relief flashes through Wade's features and he leans back in his chair. "You—you believe me?"

Sheriff Gordon mimics Wade's position, shifting back into his chair. "I'm not sure what in the hell I believe at the moment. But what I do know is this... We've had almost a dozen graves desecrated over the past few weeks and all of them are from folks who were recently deceased. It's turning into a circus as we try to calm down their next of kin. To top it all off, I've had not one, but two accounts from citizens saying they've seen the dead wandering the streets. We've had to take two of them down because they were terrorizing anyone in their path. So, I'm a tad inclined to follow up on your story here. Especially since it would mean there could be more out there."

Wade's eyelashes flutter and his mouth drops open. "Others have seen them?"

"Didn't I just say that?" he says, lowering his eyebrows.

"That's actually kind of a relief. I was beginning to feel like they were being sent after me," Wade says, dropping his gaze to the table.

"Now, why would you think that?" The sheriff asks, leaning in again.

Wade shakes his head. "No reason, I guess. It just sorta felt that way when it was my grandpa's columbarium that was desecrated—and then to have the revenants come after me when I was out there."

I bite my lip, settling my gaze on my hands. The fact that his dead grandpa is locked in the boathouse, when he should be nothing but ashes, hasn't been mentioned.

"Well, I think it's safe to say this isn't about you, Mr. Hoffman. But I'd sure appreciate any insights you might have about this. Now, you said the dead attacked you. Do you remember anything specific about it? Or who they were?"

"There were two of them and they sorta just came out of nowhere," Wade says, his gaze softening as he tries to remember. "I was just there and it was like they were drawn to me. I ran, trying to find someplace where I could find safety, but there wasn't anything. But the revenants..." Wade takes a deep breath, shivering.

"Yes?" The sheriff urges.

Wade's silver eyes flick upward and land on the sheriff's freckled face. "They were *relentless*."

"How do you mean?" he asks, narrowing his gaze.

"They wouldn't stop coming and they were fast. Way faster than I expected from watching TV."

The sheriff nods. "Television is usually a load of crap. At least, that's almost always the case. So, tell me, what happened next? You're obviously still here. How did you stop them?"

"The first one took me down to the ground. I stopped it by shoving a wreath stand through his—" Wade holds up a finger, pointing to the location beneath his jaw. He shudders again. "So, at least 'The Walking Dead' was right about that one."

Sheriff Gordon nods, but his expression has turned stone cold. "And the other one?"

"It was crawling on the ground and I managed to topple a headstone over. The weight crushed it."

"I see," he says, tipping his head in acknowledgement. "From what I gather, the bodies were disintegrating when they were discovered. Any idea how that could have happened?"

Wade shakes his head. "No, not really. I mean, whatever magic animated them in the first place must have been negated because that did happen quickly when we—I mean, when I was still there."

I can't help but inhale sharply at the slip, but I cover my nose, acting like I have to sneeze. Wade's eyes widen, but he refuses to look my direction.

"That must have been very difficult for you. You didn't know either of them, you know, personally...did you?"

"No, sir. Neither one."

The sheriff's chin tips upward and he rubs at the spot just under his bottom lip. "Now, I'm not a super, but I've worked with plenty. I don't suppose you happen to know of anyone with the kind of power it takes to do something like this? Resurrect the dead and reanimate them?"

Wade's lips tug downward as he shakes his head slightly. "No, I'm new in town."

"Okay, I think you said that, didn't you? Now, we've got a special investigator coming in who handles this sort of thing. Or so I'm told. People higher up the pay grade than myself seem to think there's only a couple of different types of supers who have the ability to pull this off."

My eyes widen and I sit up straighter.

"Now, I'm not sure how many people we have in the town with the ability, but we do have Windhaven Academy working with us to narrow down the list as we speak," the sheriff says nonchalantly. "What kind of abilities do you possess, Mr. Hoffman, if you don't mind my asking?"

Wade's nostrils flare with his tense inhalation. "None. At least, none as of yet. The abilities in my family are latent, but I was told it didn't matter to the academy."

"I see," he says, tipping his head. "And what kind of powers would they be? You know, if they were active..."

"They're more psychic in nature," he says softly, refusing to look my way. "I'd be able to sense certain energies."

I raise my eyebrows. That's more information about his powers than I've gotten.

Is that why he and Dominic seem to clash?

"Yeah, that's not quite the sort of powers we're looking for—from what I'm told. We need someone with ties to heavier elemental magic. Necromancy, earth or water magic, that sort of thing." Narrowing his eyes, Sheriff Gordon's discerning gaze suddenly lands squarely on me. "And what kind of abilities do *you* have, Ms. Blackwood?"

CHAPTER 15

ALL EYES ARE ON

The last thing I expected when we went into the Windhaven PD was to divert suspicion from Wade by drawing their attention to me. Now that Sheriff Gordon knows I'm the town's only necromancer, the likelihood of this going away anytime soon is pretty much nonexistent. Plus, if they decide to do just a little bit of digging and find out that we have Wade's dead grandpa locked up in my boathouse, there's going to be hell to pay.

And, if that wasn't enough, the entire school is giving me a wide berth now, too. I know exactly how Wade was feeling the first few weeks of school.

"This sucks," I blurt out, taking a seat in the commons area beside Wade. I lean forward, placing my face in my hands. "I can't believe I'm a suspect."

Wade shifts out of the lounge chair beside me and places a hand on my back. "Person of interest—don't get excited now."

I shoot him a sideways glance and cover my face again with my hands.

He chuckles under his breath. "Don't worry, Autumn. It'll get sorted out."

I look up, cutting him off with my expression. "Just a couple of days ago, you said I was nuts for having faith in things getting sorted out. Now that roles are reversed..."

"Now that roles are reversed, I *know* it's true. Neither one of us will stop until we figure out who's really behind this. Besides, I'm not out of the water yet. If that video goes public, I'm sure I'll be back in the central ring of rumors, no matter what Sheriff Gordon thinks. The only good news is that the feds are supposed to be here today. The sooner they get started, the sooner they'll realize neither one of us had anything to do with this," Wade says, crouching down beside me and pulling my hands into his.

His eyes plead with mine, and I can't help but sigh.

"Wade, you didn't even tell Sheriff Gordon I was with you in the cemetery. If they find out, and think we kept it from them, they'll think I was trying to hide it," I mutter, rolling my eyes to the ceiling.

"Trying to hide what?" Cat asks, practically bouncing in from the hallway.

I narrow my gaze and quirk an eyebrow. "Why are you so happy?"

"I've had a lovely day, thank you for asking. I've been holed up in my room, working on some missing assignments and thank the Lord, it's helped. My grades are finally pulling back up and I feel more like myself than I have in *ages*," she says, smiling broadly. Plopping down into a seat across from us, her dark eyes flit from me to Wade and back again. "So, what's up with you, Ms. Gloomypants?"

"Ugh," I groan. "Haven't you heard already? I don't even know where to start."

Standing up, she plants herself down on the armrest of my chair and chuckles. "At the beginning. I feel like it's been forever since we chatted. I'm totally lost."

"That makes two of us," I say, shaking my head. "There's so much..."

"Actually, this isn't really the best place to talk about things," Wade says, keeping his tone low. His eyes dart around the commons, landing on a small group of people in the corner who are huddled together. Every few moments, one of them looks in our direction, then returns to their group.

"Wonderful," I say, slumping back into the chair.

"Seriously, guys...what am I missing?" Cat asks, concern now sweeping her features.

"Autumn's a person of interest in the grave desecrations," Wade says in such a hushed tone I'm surprised Cat can even hear him.

"No—" she blurts out, shock clear across her face.

Wade and I both nod.

"Well, that's just the most ridiculous thing I ever... I mean, why would they even..." she says, stumbling over her words.

"Whoever it is, they're not playing around with the graves or trying to rob them. They're actually summoning the dead," I say, pressing my lips into a thin line. "And guess whose family is the only one known for necromancy in this town?"

"*Shit.*" Cat says, dropping her shoulders.

"Yeah," I mutter, closing my eyes.

Cat sighs. "So, what do we do? I mean, what do you want to do?"

I shrug. "What can I do? I need to let the authorities figure it out. The more I profess my innocence, the more people think I'm lying. Especially since they assumed it was Wade first."

Colton walks into the commons, clearly looking for his sister, as his eyes scan the space and land first on her. His expression falters when he sees the two of us, but he drops his chin and shuffles over anyway.

My insides clench. The last thing I need is something else to stress out over right now and having Colton in close proximity is sure to boost my stress levels.

Colton shoves his hands into his pockets and stops a few feet away. "Hey," he says, tipping his chin upward.

Wade's back stiffens, but he tips his chin in return. Even without knowing about Colton's kiss, the tension rolling off of him is palpable. I swear, if things weren't so complicated right now, I'd come clean and deal with the ramifications.

"Hi, Colt," I say, feigning a smile.

Colton's lips curve upward ever so slightly, then he drops his gaze to the ground. "You ready, Cat?" he asks, refusing to look up.

"Did you hear about Autumn?" Cat says, ignoring the question.

Colton's curiosity gets the better of him and he glances up, placing his discerning eyes on me. "What about her?"

Cat curls her pointer finger, urging him to come closer. He does as she requests, leaning forward until his face is inches from hers.

"The police think Autumn is a suspect in this whole grave vandalism thing. Can you believe it?" she whispers.

Colton's eyes widen and he snickers. His eyes shift from Cat to Wade, then land squarely on me. "That's —*preposterous*."

"Right?" She nods her head in agreement. "Evidently, the cops think whoever's doing this is raising the dead and she's the only known necromancer in town."

Shaking his head, Colton crams his hands beneath his arms. "Why—why would they think a necromancer has anything to do with this?"

Cat's lips press into a thin line and she quirks an eyebrow. "Really? Did you not hear the part about the dead being raised?"

"Yeah, but did they come back to life? Or are they just..."

"Revenants?" I say, unable to help myself.

Colton's eyes narrow and his eyebrows crease in confusion.

"Zombies," Wade reiterates, entering the fray for the first time.

"Yeah," Colton says, swallowing hard, "that's what I meant."

"They're definitely revenants," I mutter.

My gaze flits to the group in the corner. The five of them are all turned in our direction, raptly listening to our conversation. Anger flares through me and I stand up.

"What are you looking at? Huh?" I spit, my fists clenching at my side. "Don't you have anything better to do with your time?"

The two girls edge away, clearly startled by my outburst. The three guys, on the other hand, stand up, immediately going to the defense of the ladies in their circle.

"Haven't you done enough, necro? You all should be behind bars," a large redhead says, squaring his shoulders. His dark-brown eyes flash as he shoots sideways glances at the two guys by his side.

The brunette to his left crosses his arms over his broad chest and tips his chin in approval while the sandy blond adjusts his glasses, clearly not looking for a fight but not willing to back down, either.

"Done enough?" I sputter, narrowing my gaze and taking a step toward them.

Suddenly, both Wade and Cat are on their feet, standing just steps behind me.

"And how the hell would you know what she's done?" Wade growls.

"She hasn't done anything wrong," Colton says, taking a step out in front of the rest of us. His fist are clenched at his sides, and the chairs around us begin to rattle.

The guys across the room take a small step back, startled.

"What the hell, man? We've got no beef with you," the sandy blond says.

"Colton," I warn, stepping forward and placing a hand on his arm. Suddenly, I feel the strange, warming sensation again as the iridescent blue and orange flames start to engulf my hand. Startled, I pull it back.

Immediately, the rattling ceases.

I twist around, hoping Wade didn't catch it. Luckily, his attention is centered solely on the group ahead of us. My shoulders relax slightly as I turn back to the threat across the room.

"If she hasn't done anything wrong, why does she need everyone else to stand up for her? Huh? We heard about you, Blackwood. All last semester you pretended you had no idea you were a necromancer. What bullshit. Your family practically coined the term and you didn't know. Then you go and bring this one back," the burly redhead says, jabbing a finger toward Cat. "So, what...is this some sort of publicity stunt? Or are you really just one of those kinds of people who need to have all the attention all the time?"

I roll my eyes.

"You don't even know her," Colton says, taking another step forward.

"Neither do you," Wade says, a hint of rage boiling beneath his tone.

Looking over my shoulder, I shoot him a look and mouth, "What the hell?"

Wade ignores my question, instead taking a step around me so he can put himself between me and the other group.

The testosterone rolling through the entire commons is so thick I want to barf. I shake my head, unable to deal with any more of it. It's as if their egos are what matters in all of this and it's sickening.

Without another word to any of them, I spin around, pick up my backpack, and walk out.

There's literally nothing I can say or do to change anyone's minds, and sitting in the middle of a boy battle is only going to make things worse. Besides, I have more important things to worry about right now. Like what the hell am I going to do about Wade's dead grandpa?

Cat chases after me, rushing to catch up. "Autumn, wait. Just ignore those guys. They're—"

"Not now, Cat. I really can't deal with any more of this shit," I say, swiping my hand through the air and cutting her off.

"I know you, though. I know the good you strive for. People will believe whatever they want to. Especially if it means getting attention for themselves. But they're not who matters here," she says, her eyebrows tipping in the middle as she tries to reach out for me.

I shake my head, refusing to stop. Instead, I push open the door to the building and keep walking. When I reach the bottom of the large stone staircase leading to the parking lot, both Wade and Colton burst through the doors behind us.

"Autumn," Wade calls out, rushing to make his way to me. "*Dru*, stop. Please."

Despite myself, I pull up short. My anger boils over and I spit, "What, Wade? What do you want? Do you want to beat your chest some more? Knock me over the head with your caveman club and drag me back home?"

Wade takes a step back, clearly wounded.

I pinch the bridge of my nose and sigh. "Look, I'm sorry. I didn't mean that. I just can't handle all of this right now. Not on top of everything else."

God, I wish I was anywhere but here. Anywhere but under the scrutiny of everyone.

Other students filter out of the school, some of them eyeing us suspiciously as they walk by. I do my best to ignore them, but I know if I stand here too much longer, I'm going to flip my shit. Big time.

Colton bounds down the remaining couple of steps,

reaching out for my arm the way Cat had. "Autumn, don't be mad. We were all just trying to—"

I try to pull my arm out of the way, but it's too late. His hand comes into contact with my elbow and almost immediately the familiar iridescent flames erupt across my arm and over his hand.

"Get off of me," I blurt out, pulling my arm back from him.

But it's too late. I look over to Wade's wide eyes and white face. He scoffs, taking another step back.

Walking away from Colton, I take a step toward Wade, my hands out in front of me. "Wade…"

He shakes his head, and his lips tug downward. "So, guess that's still a thing."

"It's not a *thing*," I say, trying to ignore the tremors rolling through my limbs. "You already know it's just—"

"What's not a thing? What are you talking about?" Colton says behind me.

"Guys," Cat warns. "You heard the woman. Honestly, the two of you are ridiculous. She doesn't need any peacocking right now. Both of you need to back the eff up." Her jaw sets and her dark eyes flash furiously.

Any trace of the odd version of her I talked to in the woods is gone, and I can't help but be somewhat relieved. The last thing I need right now is to also be sought after because of a resurrection gone wrong.

Wade's jaw clenches and he steps around me. "Why don't you just keep moving, Colton? Don't you get it? She's already got a boyfriend and I'm not going *anywhere*."

Colton holds his chin up, flitting his gaze from Wade to me. His lips curve into a small smirk and he whispers, "We'll see about that."

CHAPTER 16
THE JIG IS UP

The next few days fly by as if they've been sucked into some sort of fast-forward time warp. If there's one thing I've learned, it's being under suspicion is not conducive to being in the present moment. I almost wish this renowned psychic would hurry up and make it here. If he's worth a grain of salt, maybe he can actually prove I had nothing to do with any of this and find the actual asshats who are.

"Did you hear the latest? More of the dead have risen. Still all freshly dead. They're pretty convinced there's a spell on the two cemeteries," Wade says, joining me in the overcrowded hallway.

I hike my backpack higher onto my shoulder. "Wonderful. How'd you hear that?"

"Chelsea," Wade says, pushing open the door to the cafeteria and holding it wide. "She's been keeping a pulse on things for us."

I shoot him a sideways glance, trying to suppress the flush of jealousy. "You mean *for you*."

Wade's dark eyebrows merge. "No...pretty sure I meant *us*. What's up with you today?"

"N-nothing. I just want this all to be over. Sorry," I say, shaking my head and walking through the open doorway.

"I get it," Wade says, grabbing a tray and making his way through the line. "Let me know if there's anything you want me to do, okay?"

Shooting him a halfhearted smile, I nod and follow behind him in a daze. Truthfully, I'm not really even sure if I want to eat. My appetite has pretty much gone on hiatus during all of this, replaced instead by an insatiable appetite for worry.

What if they can't prove me innocent? What if I can't convince them? Could I end up going to prison?

I can't go to prison.

We make our way through the line, and I barely manage to go through the motions. Wade and I find an open table by the windows. I shove my backpack to the far side of the bench, and as we settle in, I stare down at my tray. I somehow managed to grab an orange juice, a slice of pizza, and a handful of green peppers. I don't even like green peppers.

Pushing the tray aside, I stare out the window. Even without looking, I feel the weight of the stares from people all around us.

"Not hungry?" Wade asks, taking a bite of his own slice of pizza.

At least he's gotten his appetite back.

I shake my head, letting my gaze filter out across the room. The majority of people have the decency to at least divert their eyes when I glance their way. There are, however, the few who lean in, conversing to someone beside them as they point in our direction.

Rather than turning away, I force myself to look each one of them in the eye. I refuse to back down and shrink from their accusatory glares.

A few tables back, near one of the enormous stone pillars holding up the space, a student catches my eye. The bright pink chunk of hair tucked behind her left ear is the first thing to capture my attention, but it's her discerning blue eyes that send chills straight through me. It's like they could rip me apart and spit me back out. She sits completely alone, and instead of eating, her large black combat boots are propped up on the edge of the table, crossed at the ankles, as if she's simply here to make me uncomfortable.

Shuddering at the chill creeping up my spine, I raise an eyebrow and set my jaw. I don't know who this chick is, but I refuse to be the first to look away.

Oddly enough, the corners of her lips twist upward into a smirk. But she doesn't turn away. If anything, it's like she accepts the challenge.

"What are you looking at?" Wade asks, twisting his head around and surveying the sea of people.

Despite myself, I break my concentration and turn to him. "Do you see that chick? Over near the pillar, with the hot-pink hair?"

"Yeah," he mutters with a nod. "God, she looks like she could rip us to shreds."

"Right?" I say. "Well, she's been staring at us for—"

Abruptly, the chick uncrosses her legs and stands up. She pulls her ultra-light-blond hair into a loose ponytail, leaving the pink chunk to stray loose. Adjusting her Pink

Floyd t-shirt and the zipper edge of her grey leather jacket, she pushes in her chair as if manners in this place are actually a thing. Without a single air of embarrassment or apprehension, she walks through the cafeteria like she owns the place—and of course, directly toward us.

"Do you know her?" Wade asks in a hushed tone.

I shake my head. "I've never even seen her before. Have you?"

There's an air of power around her that I can't quite put my finger on. People move out of her way, giving her a wide berth without any verbal request or even really acknowledging they're doing it. As she reaches our booth, she grabs a chair from the nearest table, spinning it around in her hand and sliding it up to the outward-facing edge of our table.

Straddling the seat, she folds her arms across the back. "Guess the jig is up, huh?"

"Excuse me?" I say, blinking back surprise.

She sighs heavily, rolling her big blue eyes as if my question offends her. "You know, guess I've been found out. Exposed. Discovered? Are any of these words ringing a bell?" She narrows her eyes and purses her lips as she waits for a response. "Wow, what do they teach you guys in this place? They really should start with language."

My brain feels as though it's seized up and all I seem capable of doing is staring blankly in her direction.

"Who are you?" Wade asks, pushing his tray aside.

Her face brightens a bit as she turns to him, almost peering at him through her pink bangs. "You know, that is the existential question, isn't it? I mean, who are any of us, really?" She opens her arms wide, as if she's commanding the space around her in some sort of orchestrated event.

It's Wade's turn to look dumbfounded as he turns his wide, silver eyes to me.

"Okay, so I can tell the two of you aren't super-fast on the uptake, so I'll do you a favor and see if you can play catch-up. My name's Diana," she says, as if the word should be completely self-explanatory.

When neither of us make a move in acknowledgement, she exhales in exasperation, extending a hand and stealing one of my green peppers. She pops it into her mouth, then extends the same hand out to me. Without thinking, I reach forward to shake it. However, Diana places her other hand over top of mine, locking it in place. Closing her eyes, she practically pulls me off my seat as she tugs my hand in to her body.

Instantly, my entire arm hums with a strange combination of heat and static electricity, igniting a domino effect of goosebumps across my flesh. "Um, excuse me," I say, yanking my hand back.

Diana opens her eyes slowly, sitting up straighter in her chair. Evidently finished with me, she turns her piercing gaze to Wade. Her eyes flit from the top of his head downward, but she doesn't extend her hand to him.

She shakes her head and mutters, "*Angel*. How quaint."

Wade's face pales and my mouth pops open.

How in the hell did she know the pet name I have for him?

Suspicion dissipates and I lean back in my seat. "Ah... you're the world-renowned psychic we've been hearing about. No offense, but aren't you a little young?"

She's certainly not what I expected. If anything, she's got maybe a year on me, and if that's the case, there's a good chance Wade's older than her.

Again, she smirks, her eyes twinkling mischievously. "What's age got to do with anything?"

Again, it's not the response I was expecting. She clearly just likes to turn people in circles. Probably so she can make herself seem more powerful. Despite her knowing Wade's nickname, it doesn't mean she has psychic gifts that go beyond Dominic's.

What a joke.

"Well, a lot, actually. Look around you. This school is filled with people our age, all trying to learn how to master their abilities. How am I supposed to believe you can pick things up better than they can?" I say, holding back my indignation as best I can.

Diana leans forward, with an oddly gentle expression taking over her features. "And you believe a school like this is the only way to hone those abilities, do you?"

"Well…" Sorta. But with the way she's looking at me, I'm inclined to keep that to myself.

"Diana, if you are who you say you are, then you'll have to give us something more to go on. No offense, but this is a college campus, and everyone here has it in for us at the moment. So, you'll have to forgive us if we don't take you at face value," Wade says, recovering from his initial surprise.

Diana inhales slowly through her nose, letting her gaze fall to the table then rise up to him. "I understand your hesitation, Mr. Hoffman. I do, but I'm not the one under investigation here." Diana's eyes flick to me. "She is. So, I guess what I'm trying to say is…*I'm disinclined to acquiesce to your request.*"

Wade inhales sharply and his gaze snaps over to me. I'm not sure if it's from the fact that she so bluntly said

I'm under investigation or the fact that she used a movie quote reference from one of his favorites.

She's either fishing, a genius, or actually rooting around in his brain.

"Fair enough. What do you want?" I say, turning to her.

"Don't be coy, Ms. Blackwood. You know why I'm here. I've been sent to assess your level of interaction with the local resurrections," she says, turning to me without batting an eye. "So, do you have anything you'd like to confess? Anything on your mind and weighing on you?"

"I didn't do anything—" I blurt out. Of course, the first thing that comes to mind is Cat's resurrection and the weird interaction with her in the woods.

Diana's blue eyes home in on me. "So, there *has* been a resurrection, then? Who's Cat?"

My pulse quickens, and I gape at her.

She chuckles under her breath and shakes her head.

"What are you laughing at?" I say, slamming my hands down on the table in front of me.

She tips her chin condescendingly and pats the top of my left hand. "There, there, little one. No need to get yourself worked up. You'll give yourself premature wrinkles."

"Ugh," I moan. She's just toying with me, but I'm starting to feel like a mouse who can't escape.

"See, here's the thing, kids," Diana begins, resting her forearms on the table and clasping her hands out in front of her. "There's only two ways revenants like the ones in this town can be called forth. The first one would take a magician capable of harnessing the higher vibrations of earth energies. We're talking deep, powerful magic. Not only would that take an incredible skill level of biomancy, but it also requires the use of relics very few have even heard of. Or...the more *likely* scenario is a newbie necromancer was playing around with forces beyond her capabilities and level of awareness... and who, of course, didn't know any better. Since all magicians with elemental magic get catalogued and there's no one in this area with that level of power just yet, it sorta leaves you." She shoots me a knowing look. "So, you can see our predicament. Now, let's try this again. Who's Cat?"

"Cat has nothing to do with any of this. I haven't done anything wrong. This wasn't me—"

However, a seed of doubt blossoms in my abdomen.

Could I have done this? I've even had my own doubts about her...

Diana's eyebrow arches upward, as if she hears every word in my mind. Then, she leans in close to me. "Autumn, you're gifted—naturally so, in fact. I'll give you that. Your powers have a greater capacity than you've even begun to test. It's almost as if you're afraid to. Why?"

I blink back in surprise.

I'd never even looked at it that way. Instead, I sorta feel like I don't have control of what happens. Abigail, the resurrection chamber, the revenants... I'm in reaction mode without a chance to be proactive.

Diana's tongue flicks across her lower lip and she turns to Wade. "So, you're also in the epicenter of all of this, Mr. Hoffman. What about you? Anything *on your mind?*"

His face again drains of color and he shakes his head. "No, Autumn's right. We have no idea what's causing any of this. We just want it all to be over."

Silence expands between the three of us as Diana watches every movement Wade makes with rapt attention.

"I'm not entirely certain why you're shrouding yourself with so much...*mystery*. But I'd be careful if I were you. It could be your undoing. I should know."

"What on earth are you talking about?" I say.

"Nothing you need to worry your sweet little head about," she says in the same kind of tone a grandmother uses when trying to appease a young child. "All right, let me be frank with you guys. You are both *adorably* oblivious to what's actually happening. It was clear from the moment I walked in this epicenter of hormones and magic, but even more so now that I've had some time in your energy. The problem is, the real world likes tangible proof. It's a bummer, I know. And so far, I can't offer them anything yet. I don't know who the real culprit is. For whatever reason, they're seriously shrouded. Like there's another energy blocking my way."

I lean back, breathing a sigh of relief. She doesn't think either of us did it.

"What do you need from us?" I say, tapping the edge of the table.

"I need you to cooperate with whatever comes your way. I can't protect the two of you if you're not willing to work with me," she says. "I need total honesty among everyone. But right now, you both clearly have some secrets and, while it's none of my business, I'm gettin' the vibe they're at the heart of the matter here. So, I'm going to give you a couple of days to communicate and clear the air. In the meantime, I'll do more digging. See ya around, kiddos."

I turn my gaze to Wade, my eyebrows tugging in.

What secrets does she mean?

My eyes widen and I turn back to her. Did she pick up on Colton's kiss? Oh, god...

"Needless to say, don't go anywhere. We're not done here, not by a long shot. Mkay?" Diana says, grinning like a mad woman as she stands up.

"I'm not going anywhere," I say, jutting out my chin.

"That's good. But I mean *both* of you." Turning on her heel, she walks away from the table. Her blond ponytail swings around, bobbing along as she walks.

Wade and I exchange a significant glance.

"Oh, and by the way," Diana says, turning back around, "you might wanna ignore that. It's not good news."

Wade's eyebrows tug in. "Ignore what?"

Suddenly, the sound of ringtones erupt across the cafeteria.

CHAPTER 17
SPEAK YOUR TRUTHS

I t's amazing how quickly tides can turn. I'm starting to get whiplash from it all, to be honest.

If I thought things couldn't be worse, I was certainly fooling myself. It was better when Wade was more upbeat and I had become the magnet for rumors. We'd almost forgotten about the video at the cemetery in Mistwood. After his confession to the police, we were both kinda hoping it would go away—or wouldn't be as bad at the very least. But, as promised, the video was released to the whole school and went viral in minutes.

Sitting on my bed, I glance down at my phone, watching the video of Wade toppling the tombstone for the umpteenth time. It was cut close in such a way that it looks like he was just there to damage property or desecrate bodies. Of course, that's pretty much what everyone has assumed, too.

Now, no matter what we say or do, Wade and I are both the center of suspicion with the entire student body. Even with this psychic chick, Diana, supposedly on our side, it hasn't saved us at all. In fact, I haven't heard a word from her since.

So much for her protection.

On the other hand, though, I'm beginning to think Diana's right about one thing. Maybe I don't really want these powers of life and death. When I was a kid, I wanted to fly, or turn invisible, walk through walls, or maybe have the ability to conjure portals. Hell, Cat's ability to summon fire would be better. Not necromancy. Not the ability to talk to the dead and stop them from crossing over. As much as I hate to admit it, I don't really think anyone should have the power to decide who lives and who dies.

Fighting the urge to be sick, I can't even begin to imagine who could possibly believe Wade and I would desecrate graves or damage headstones on purpose. Especially for the fun of it.

The video comes to an end and I tap out, staring at my phone's home screen.

Suddenly, a text message comes in from Mom, making me jump. I tap the message out of reflex, but regret it instantly.

Hey, sweetie. Hope your new semester is going good. Give me a call when you get a sec. I'd love to catch up. <3 Love, Mom. xxx

Besides the normal guilt, from not texting or calling as often as I should, I feel a stab of anxiety about responding. Do I lie and say it's going great? Or do I ghost her and hope she just thinks I'm busy? Neither are great options, but telling her the truth is completely out of the question.

Deciding for the lesser of two evils, I type a quick response back.

Hi Mom! Definitely. <3 I'm busy right now, but I'll call you later this week. Okay?

Tossing my phone behind me on the bed, I flop down on my back and stare at the ceiling.

This is definitely not how I envisioned my time at Windhaven Academy would go. Maybe Mom was right to be dubious about everything. So far, having abilities has brought me nothing but suspicion, pain, and heartache. If she knew, she'd probably be begging me to come back to Mistwood Point.

My phone buzzes, making the fabric beside my head vibrate, and I close my eyes, unable to deal with anything more right now. Instead, I sit up, staring at the familiar, handsome face of Wade as he tries to reach me on a call. But no matter how much I love him, I can't bring myself to answer the phone and I'm not really sure why.

He's the one person who knows better than anyone how this feels, but I need a break from thinking about it all.

My eyes sweep to the big picture window overlooking the courtyard. Snow flitters from the overcast sky, as if the clouds haven't quite decided whether or not to truly release their haul. It's still beautiful, anyway. Standing up, I walk over to the window, wishing I could be as carefree as one of the snowflakes.

Suddenly, a cold shiver courses through me and I pull my arms in tight, unable to get warm. Looking over my shoulder, I search for the source of the draft and there, standing a few feet behind me, is Abigail.

Her face is forlorn, but her lips curve upward when I lock eyes with her.

"I apologize for my intrusion. I did not mean to disturb you," she says, her voice barely a whisper. "You seemed burdened."

I attempt a smile. "That's an understatement."

Abigail moves toward me, her dress barely touching the ground. At first, she doesn't say a word, but her forehead wrinkles, betraying her own thoughts.

Nervous energy rolls through my torso and I can't help but worry about what's on her mind.

"Autumn, I am quite certain you don't always understand my delivery of things with utmost importance. I wish I could be more forthright, but certain wisdom requires a more delicate approach," she says, rubbing the top side of her right hand with her fingertips. "Our family, our legacy...and it is more fickle than it appears to the casual observer. At times, it comes at great cost."

Shaking my head, I sit down on the window seat. "I'm beginning to understand that."

"There's still so much you do not yet know and so much I wish I could tell you..."

I narrow my gaze, confused. "Then what's stopping you?"

Her lips press into a thin line and her gaze falls to the ground.

"So, you can't say?"

Narrowing her eyes, she tilts her head toward the doorway to the resurrection chamber. "Follow me, would you?"

Without walking to the door and opening it like a live person would, she fades from the room as she turns to face the door leading down to the resurrection chamber. It's almost as if her body is sucked through the entryway one particle at a time, floating away like those snowflakes falling from the sky.

Taking a deep breath, I stand up and walk over to the bed to grab my phone so I have a flashlight with me. It's been months since I last went into the resurrection chamber. In fact, not since the night we brought Cat back. I just haven't been able to bring myself to go back down there.

I pull the door open and walk down the wooden steps, suddenly consumed by the feelings and sensations I was consumed with that night. The panic and fear...and *power*. That's something I haven't felt since. If anything, I've felt pretty powerless lately.

When my feet hit the sandy floor of the resurrection chamber, the room is already lit dimly by the magical torches around the room. I cram my phone into my pocket.

Abigail hovers in the center of the drawn pentacle, still left in the middle of the room. My gaze is drawn to the dark stains in the sand; remnants of the ritual. As I get closer to Abigail, the energy in the room shifts, vibrating at a level that makes the hairs on the back of my neck stand on end.

"Come," Abigail urges, rolling her fingers and beckoning me forth.

Somewhat reluctantly, I walk forward until I'm standing in the center of the pentagram with her.

"Behold this space. What do your examinations yield?" she asks quietly.

Swallowing hard, I turn around and inspect the room.

"Well, it's old," I begin, eyeing the haphazardly built stone walls and dirt floor. "There are no windows other than the ones in the stairwell..."

"Good. What else?" she urges.

I scratch my temple, feeling utterly silly doing this with a ghost. "I see the pentacle of salt, the blood, and other items from the ritual we performed for Cat."

"Veritably. Go on."

I straighten my shoulders, shooting her a sideways glance. "There are torches—like the ones that you'd see inside tunnels or outside old buildings. Only they're not real."

She chuckles and the smile cracking her face brings a certain beauty to her features. "Be not dissuaded. They are utterly real. Your perception of reality has yet to be adjusted to what truly is," she says, taking a step outside the circle. "Regard this space with a critical eye. What more do you detect?"

Pressing my lips tightly, I do as she asks. My awareness expands outward, focusing on the sensations of the room, and I involuntarily shudder. "There's an energy to the room I guess I haven't really taken notice of before. It's like walking into a walk-in freezer, only I'm not really cold."

"Ah, now your senses are beginning to swell," she grins. "Press onward. What else?"

Shaking my head, I turn to Abigail. "There isn't a

whole lot more in this room. I'm not sure what else you're—"

"Close your eyes. Forego sight in the typical fashion and tell me what you witness," Abigail says, her face lighting up from some kind of excitement, or maybe amusement at my attempts.

"I don't—"

She raises a ghostly hand. "Humor me and do as I request, Autumn. Please."

Stretching my neck and relaxing my shoulders, I close my eyes. I feel somewhat ridiculous standing in the middle of the room with my eyes shut, but after a moment, the feeling dissipates. Instead, it's replaced with a strange sense of calm. The anxiety and high-voltage energy washes away, as if I were suddenly plunged into a cool spring. I can't help but hold my breath, curious to whatever may come next.

"You have been grievously tainted by the sights of your modern era. I have found it to be a most dreadful affliction at times. Instead of residing in your gifts, allowing them to become a part of you, you lose your ability to be drawn into the eternal laws of magic. I suspect this is through much conditioning outside our inner sanctum, but regardless..." Her voice drifts off. When she speaks again, she is closer. "Keeping your eyes closed, cast a wider ken. Tell me, what feelings arise in you first?"

"A sense of calm, for starters," I say, raising my eyebrows, but keeping my eyes shut.

"That is but a side effect of turning inward, calming the mind to embark into stillness. Being what we are requires a certain amount of strength and concentration. It also demands our intentional efforts to be but one with our gifts. Necromancy is not simply the resurrection of another. It is about immersion beyond the veil—to the heart from where all energy springs. We cannot do this properly without learning how to calm the storm raging within our own minds," she says, circling around me. "You will be your own worst enemy if you cannot quell its beckoning. You must not allow yourself to be tormented by it."

I shift awkwardly, unsure what to say to something like that.

"Move beyond the serenity. What senses entice you forth?"

Inhaling slowly, I allow the stillness to overcome me until everything else is completely tuned out. The room falls deafeningly silent and it's as if the whole world falls completely away. Then, almost like a single candle was lit inside the darkness, behind my eyelids, I can make out the entire room. Only, rather than seeing it in three dimensions, it's more like looking through thermal imaging or an infrared camera. Some areas around the room are a cool blue, all the way up to a deeper cyan. Then there are areas around the room that are red, orange, and even yellow. Turning my head to face the ground, the salt glows a bright, crystal white, but the blood splatter shows up as an intense, fluorescent yellow.

Curious, keeping my eyes closed, I bend down and touch it.

"Speak your truths. What observations do you witness?" Abigail says softly.

"Colors—everything is bright," I say, standing back up.

"Exemplary." There's a hint of satisfaction hidden in the tone of her voice. "Your gifts have returned with haste. Manifold objects require that you must be in alignment with their essence before they reveal themselves. I am quite sure you can appreciate there is much in this world that hath not yet shown themselves unto you."

I open my eyes, glancing over at Abigail. After realizing I can see spirits who are trapped, it's definitely occurred to me once or twice that there are many levels to reality.

"I do," I say, nodding.

Abigail clasps her hands in front of her body and smiles. "Dimensions overlap each other repeatedly. Sometimes, the only way to detect a rift is by honing our abilities. Other times, we require tools to be one with the universal energies. I am certain you have calculated that you have been miraculously gifted with both my ability for resurrection and Warren's ability to behold the unseen. I believed this to be true from very early on, but I had no way of being certain. It was not a proven theory until your successful reinsertion of the Gilbert girl's soul."

"That's a good thing, though. Right?" I say, quirking an eyebrow.

Abigail tilts her head to the side, considering. "It may have its benefits."

"Well, super," I say, making a face.

"Direct your attention inward yet again and tell me what it is you sense about this chamber. From whence did it arise?"

"Why?" I ask, wondering what she's trying to get at.

"We shall see," she says, raising an eyebrow expectantly.

"Fine," I mutter under my breath. Again, I close my eyes and turn inward. I shut down all of my other senses until the calm returns and the strange colors flicker to life inside my inner sight.

"Have you regained the clarity of sight?" Abigail says from somewhere behind me.

I nod. "Yes."

"Good. Now, turn widdershins very slowly with a watchful eye. Tell me what impressions you get of this chamber from this sacred level."

"Widdershins? What does that even mean?" I say, shaking my head.

"Anti-clockwise."

"You mean counter-clockwise," I mumble.

Swallowing hard, I use my internal sight to look around the room. The stones on the wall vibrate in varying degrees of colors, some brighter than others. As I rotate a little more to my left, I can make out the stairwell and the dimming light from the window. It appears as a greyish radiance, bursting out from the edge of the stone wall. Continuing counter-clockwise, I view the back wall and the myriad stones and mortar work. Flashes of centuries' worth of memories begin to flicker through my mind's eye, flooding past more quickly than I can keep up.

Shaking my head, I turn again to my left. The memories continue to flood in, and I raise my hands to my head, trying to stop the dizzying sensation.

"There's so much residual energy. It's almost...too much," I say, trying to tune it out.

"Many lives have come and gone in this chamber. Its echo can certainly be deafening for someone unfamiliar to its pull," Abigail agrees. "Allow your senses to dive deeper. Their calling will cease."

Nodding, I try to submerge myself through the energy to find a sense of calm. When the images and information slow, I turn again, sweeping my internal gaze across the remaining wall, and the memories and visions abruptly cease. Instead, the energy is replaced by an intense level of tranquility—more potent than anything I've ever felt.

"What's happening here?" I say, reaching out with my left hand as I walk forward from the circle. Despite having my eyes closed, I can see where I'm walking as clearly as if they were open. When I reach the wall, I place my hands on the stones, unable to pick up on any energies at all from them.

"Speak your truths," Abigail urges.

"There's—" I begin, unable to form words with the level of insights coming at me. Despite having no immediate energy signature, there is still a web of magic that blankets the wall. I inhale sharply, realizing what it is I'm sensing. "There's something behind this wall."

"Indeed...*there is*."

CHAPTER 18
A WELLSPRING OF VENERATION

Surprised by the revelation, I open my eyes, and turn around to face Abigail. Only, she's gone.

"Abigail?" I call out, stumbling back from the wall. My voice echoes off of the stones and even without using my extra senses, I can tell she's not here anymore.

Sighing to myself, I return my attention to the wall. I run my fingertips over the stones, trying to understand what makes them so different. In this low light, they look exactly the same as any other stone here. The shapes, textures, and colors are all the same.

An intense reaction settles in the pit of my stomach. It's like a strange form of déjà vu. Only instead of settling in my head, it's like a punch in the gut.

There's something so familiar about all of this, but I can't put my finger on why.

Overcome with the sudden urge to see what's on the other side, I claw at the stones, trying to find one that's loose enough to pull it free. It only takes one to give way and the whole thing starts to crumble under my touch. I pull the stones free, listening to them pepper the ground, as I let them drop unceremoniously to the dirt floor.

When I've yanked enough of them to create a small opening, I bend down to get a better view. Ice-cold air rushes at me and I take a small step back, shuddering uncontrollably. Then, I hunch down to peer inside again. It's hard to see anything. Beyond the edges of the hole, it's pitch black. In fact, it's the kind of darkness you only see when you close your eyes—or when you're underground.

I close my eyes and call out, "Abigail? A little help here?"

My heart thumps unevenly in my chest as I wait for a response. When nothing happens, I stand back up, chewing on my lower lip.

Do I go in? What was the point of showing me this and vanishing? Is it a test?

"Dammit," I curse under my breath.

Pulling out my cell phone from my pocket, I tap the screen to pull up the flashlight. There are fifteen texts and two missed calls from Wade, but I swipe them away. Curiosity is getting the better of me and I have to know what's going on now. I'll call him back as soon as I see what's on the other side of this wall.

Pressing the flashlight icon, the bright LED light erupts from the other side of my phone. Bending in again, I position the light so it pierces the darkness beyond. At first, not much is visible as the light expands into the emptiness.

A knowing washes over me and I realize if this is a test, I'll have to do it with these new abilities. At least, that's what makes the most sense.

Lowering my eyebrows, I shut off the flashlight, then

put my phone back in my pocket. Closing my eyes, I settle into the new sight I'd been practicing with Abigail. However, I find that connecting with the stillness is more difficult now without her guidance. With the exception of the rush of cool air, the energy beyond the opening is completely still. There's almost an undercurrent of reverence that I can't quite put my finger on.

Interestingly, it only makes me want to see what's inside even more.

Trembling slightly, I pull a few more stones free, so there's enough room for me to step through. When the opening is big enough, I hold onto the stones around the edge. Then, I plant one foot on the other side of the wall, and crouch down, leaving the resurrection chamber to enter the other side.

As if walking through an energetic waterfall, my body vibrates from head to toe. In a weird way, it feels like it's simultaneously grounded and floating. Even though that makes absolutely no sense. The energy then settles into a quaking sensation in the pit of my stomach. When I'm fully rooted on the other side, the chill air subsides, giving way to more stillness.

Exhaling slowly, I close my eyes.

Come on, Autumn. What do you see?

Unable to stop my core from shaking, I deliberately take three deep, cleansing breaths to center myself. The inhalations do exactly as I'd hoped and my shoulders relax.

Settling into the stillness, I perk my ears, trying to pick up on any sounds inside this new chamber. When nothing is evident, I relax a bit more, feeling safer in the space. Almost instantly, I sink into the calmness and serenity reverberating around me—then past it into the next level.

The vibrant colors erupt behind my closed lids. Without seeing the space in any form of light, I can tell this section is not another room. Instead, it's a wide tunnel. Which must have been why it was hard to see anything with the flashlight.

Feeling braver, I take a few steps forward. The ground beneath my feet feels like it's made up of the same sand as the resurrection chamber, but it's smoother somehow; not nearly as worn. My feet practically carry themselves as I go farther. Relying only on this sight, I continue to walk ahead, a few feet at a time, until the tunnel reaches an abrupt end.

Fighting the desire to open my eyes and turn on the flashlight, I settle into the peace of the space, trying to understand it. I can't put my finger on why, but there's something utterly beautiful in the undercurrent of this tunnel. I practically hear music in the upper vibrations.

When I reach the end, I stop to take in as much information as these new senses can gather. The tunnel's end is a large stone archway and from what my mind's eye can see, there are ancient symbols—or perhaps ancient writing—that decorates the sides and across the lintel. They glow bright white, with a soft, almost mystical tint of purple that flickers like smoke around their edges.

I move closer, trying to get a better view of them.

Suddenly, the hairs on the back of my neck and arms prick up, and my body stiffens. I get the distinct impression I'm being watched.

"Abigail?" I call out, my voice quivering.

Stumbling backward from the archway, my enhanced vision drops, and I'm plunged back into the ordinary, all-encompassing darkness. Fumbling for my phone, my heart leaps into my throat when I realize it's not there.

"Shit," I mutter, trying to decide whether to drop to my knees and look for it, or run back the way I came.

A cold rush blows past me, rustling my hair, and my back involuntarily goes ramrod straight. My pulse pounds in my ears and I curse myself for being too curious for my own good. I should've responded to Wade. He could have been my backup. Now, no one knows where I am or what I'm even doing.

Stupid.

Spinning around, I try to figure out how far I've come. At the far end, I can barely make out the small entrance I'd created in the wall. Forcing myself to settle down, I turn counter-clockwise and close my eyes again. If there's anything here, I should be able to see it. Right?

I reach my senses out again, trying to tap into it as quickly as possible.

A low rumbling sound, almost like a growl, echoes in the darkness, making me jump.

"Hello?" I whisper, simultaneously hoping to be answered by Abigail, or not at all.

As quickly as the sensation of being watched arose, it vanishes, dropping me again into a sense of calm and peace. I exhale in a soft gasp, as I crouch down, and push my inner vision outward.

Suddenly, as if a light switch was flipped, torches ignite along the walls of a large cylindrical space beyond the hallway's arch.

Groping at my chest, I sit down completely on my butt, exhaling in relief.

Abigail stands in the middle of the circular room, her

arms raised and spread out wide. In this light, she appears even more corporeal than I've ever seen her. It's almost as if she's really here. When our eyes connect, she drops her hands and smiles.

"You were deemed worthy," she says, walking toward me.

"Um, sure?" I say, rising to a stand and taking a step into the cylindrical room. "That was kinda dramatic, don't you think?"

"Perhaps," she says, tilting her head in agreement. "But I did not make the rules."

Along the stone walls, dozens of intricately carved stone archways adorn the space, all leading off in other directions like spokes on a wheel. From this room, each archway is adorned with more stone carvings and symbols, each different, but beautifully done. On the ground, the sand leading in from each of the the tunnels makes way for larger stone slabs, each placed in a circular pattern around the room, with a single large stone in the center. It has its own unique carving on it and pulsates with an energy that draws my eyes to and makes me want to touch it.

"What is this place?" I ask, walking in circles, trying to take it all in.

Abigail watches me intensely, but raises a knowing eyebrow. "Many years back, well before the manor came into being, this sacred space was constructed. We know not by whom. We knew only that it is a wellspring of veneration for those who have come and gone before us. Those like us, and not, at the same time. When Warren and I were summoned here, we were beckoned by something much stronger than ourselves. It was the deep, powerful longing of this place, as it desired greatly for keepers who would preserve its sanctity."

I narrow my eyes. "You're saying this space has a mind of its own?"

Abigail tilts her head, considering. "Consciousness, yes, perhaps it does. The energies that converge here, long deeply for tranquility. Not only for itself, but for the souls who have been laid to rest in its embrace."

"Ah," I say, taking a step back as realization washes over me. "We're in the catacombs."

A smile spreads across Abigail's features, lighting her face in a way I've never seen. She almost looks...alive.

I shake my head, running my hand through my hair. "I should have guessed. I mean, Wade even mentioned the entrance could be inside. It just didn't think anyone would hide it in the house."

Walking slowly in a counter-clockwise movement, I peer down each spoke, trying to get a better idea of what lay beyond. Unfortunately, just like with the hallway before Abigail's help, the darkness beyond is all encompassing.

"Autumn, I must stress something of utmost importance. It was imperative that you understand that you, and you alone, were given access to this sacred space. These catacombs are a safe haven for those seeking sanctuary, but a labyrinth for those without the gift of tranquility found within our bloodline. It is essential you come to this understanding," Abigail whispers, her figure suddenly by my side.

"So, only people who are related to you can come in here? Why?" I ask, confused.

Abigail's expression falters and her lips tug downward. "This place—its magical powers are vast. It will do anything to protect itself and those within its embrace. As it should. Its importance is paramount. So, to speak plainly, yes. Your tie to us brings you protection. But it's more than this. Should someone enter and not be deemed worthy, their soul will be lost within the labyrinth, unable to ever find a way out. There are some who would call it Purgatory."

"That seems harsh. I mean, how would you know if you were worthy? Is there some sort of alarm before you get too far?" I say, startled. "Is that why the entrance was hidden?"

"Indeed, it is."

"Great," I mutter. "And now, I've just opened it."

Abigail's eyes twinkle and she takes another step toward me. "There are but two rules for entrance to these catacombs. One must be deemed capable of passing the threshold of worthiness, as is the majority of our bloodline. Or..."

I hold her gaze and my breath as I wait for her to finish.

"Or?" I say, urging her on.

Her eyebrows weave together and her lips tug into a frown. "Or, one must be touched by death."

CHAPTER 19
GATHER YOUR ALLIANCES

Obviously, the catacombs aren't meant for the living. That would sort of defeat the purpose. But the way she said it sent chills down my spine.

"So, what happens if someone who *is* living enters?" I ask, unable to help myself. "When you say Purgatory, you mean they'll be trapped between the living and—?"

Abigail's face is forlorn as she says, "As previously mentioned, there are safeguards to this sacred space. Not all who pass the threshold are taken into Purgatory's embrace. Some are simply lost until they can find a way out. For others, their price may be much higher."

"A higher cost than having your soul trapped in Purgatory?" I gape at her. "What could possibly be a higher cost than that?"

She looks over her shoulder at one of the tunnels and half-smiles. "There is much you don't know about the power coursing through your veins."

"Then, teach me—explain things to me," I beg.

"I am...and *I will*. But you must understand—not everything can be educated with such haste," she says, reaching out and hovering her hand just above my shoulder, as if unsure whether or not to place it there. After a moment, she pulls her hand back. "What say you to information brought to light of times past when the soulless walked Windhaven?"

I narrow my eyes. "You mean, did we find anything out about the revenants?"

She blinks back at me expectantly.

I raise my eyebrows and clear my throat. "Well, I found out they're called revenants, for starters. There wasn't much in the records, but Wade and I did find information pointing back to this happening thirty some odd years ago. They never caught who did it. At least not from the records we read, but..." I stop myself, unsure if I want to mention Wade's dad's involvement. Or, suspected involvement, anyway.

Abigail's head tilts slightly to the side, clearly catching my hesitation.

"But," I continue, "it hasn't happened again since. Until now, that is."

Nodding, Abigail seems appeased by this, but she circles around me. "And what of you? With the soulless arising, have you been afflicted by their presence? Do you sense their beckoning?"

"Afflicted by their presence? Like, are they coming to me?" I say, taking a deep breath and a step back. "You could say that. But sense them? No, not really. Should I be?"

A shiver skitters up my spine at the thought of sensing the revenants.

"They torment you specifically?" Abigail says, concern flashing through her features. "Are you certain?"

I shrug. "Well, sorta. They keep finding me—*us*, actually."

"Us?"

I hold her gaze for a moment. "Wade and me."

Her eyebrows knit together, and she dips her chin.

"Do you know why that is?" I ask.

Abigail's lips press into a thin line and she clasps her hands behind her back. Taking a few steps from me, her eyes flit around the space. Finally, she says, "You are a beacon for the dead. The stronger your powers grow, the more they will be drawn to you. Your presence is but a bright light in the vast abyss of darkness by which we all adhere."

"So, you're saying they find us because I'm a magnet for them?" I say, scratching my forehead.

"Perhaps," she says, raising a pointer finger in the air. "But the soulless are but empty vessels. They do not possess the qualities of the departed. They are soulless."

Frowning, I trying to make sense of what she's saying. "So, if they're empty vessels, is it just coincidence they find us?"

"Unequivocally...*no*. They are but adhering to the whispers of their maker," she says matter-of-factly.

"Their maker... So, someone else is deliberately sending them to me?" I say, my jaw slacking open.

"It would appear to be the case." She nods. "Who would wish you ill?"

I run my hands over my face. "This makes no sense whatsoever. I have no idea. Honestly, I haven't really interacted with many people. Those who I have, are friends."

"Unearthing this treachery must be paramount. You must find the perpetrator and put an end to their unnatural summoning. Then, whatever remains must be brought here to the catacombs to rest. It is the only way to quell their calling."

"If bringing them here is the only way to stop them, how were we able to stop two of them?" I ask, completely confused.

"I would not be so certain that you did," she says, casting me a knowing look that makes my skin crawl and my heart race.

Could those revenants reanimate themselves again?

Abigail sighs, walking away from me. When she reaches the archway to where I came from, her fingertips trace the symbols in the stonework. After a moment, she says, "The last time soulless roamed Windhaven—you say thirty years ago...to me, it feels but a blink of the eye..." Her gaze extends to one of the other tunnels before she walks back over to me. "It took the combined efforts of our family, the Gilberts, the Cranes...*and another* to overcome their torment. Your father, gifted though he may be, did not possess a tenth of the innate ability you bring forth. So, he had to rely on the talents of others."

The blood drains from my face and I swallow hard. That's a lot of magical power. Thirty years ago, all of those families were far more skilled than any of us. Even my father has been more in the know than myself.

"I wish Dad was home. He's gone away and I don't know when he'll be back. How am I meant to do this without him? Are you saying we'll need to round up the Gilberts and Cranes again? Or—? He could have helped with all of this," I mutter, trying to ignore the surprising well of anger from his absence and lack of technological know-how.

"Your father would be an ineffective teacher. While he may retain much knowledge, it is but abstract to him in many regards," she says. "This challenge, it is one you must face through experience. Your gifts will guide you, as will I."

"Great," I say, biting my lower lip. As if there isn't enough to worry about right now. "And how exactly are my gifts going to know what to do?"

She tips her head to the side, walking away from me again. It's like she can't stand still for longer than two seconds. "Those bodies, once reanimated, will never cease. They are abominations, and they will never stop hunting. What is worse, more will come unless you find the conjurer and put an end to their misconduct. This will require much skill on their part and yours. Based on what you've relayed, any new graves made above ground will need to be sanctified by someone with holy virtue. Someone blessed by death, but who does not wish to control it."

I snicker to myself. "Yeah, because that'll be easy to find."

"You may be surprised," she says, casting me a sideways glance.

The space between my eyebrows tightens.

"You are still so innocent, Autumn. How I do miss those days," Abigail smiles softly. "You will learn there are many others, existing on many planes, who come and go. Each caring for the delicate balance between life and death. Be not fooled. We are not the only ones graced with the ability to orchestrate the heavens."

"But..." I sigh. "Orchestrating the heavens? I don't even know what I'm doing, Abigail. This is all so new and, truth be told, my mind is kind of exploding right now. I mean, how do I know what I'm meant to do? Or how to find the help I need? I don't even know if I want any of this..."

"Do not let the challenges unhinge your confidence. Time will test you, as it always does. Here, this may be of some assistance," Abigail says, sweeping her arm out, palm side out.

Behind me, in the center of the circular room, the middle stone shifts. I turn around as a pedestal materializes before my eyes. Resting on top is the oldest-looking book I've ever seen.

"Wh—what is that?" I ask, unable to take my eyes off of it. It resonates with a power that pulsates in this small room, emitting a low hum that's both peaceful and ominous at the same time.

Abigail walks forward, gently flipping open the enormous tome. "This, my dearest Autumn, is the Blackwood family grimoire."

My eyebrows rise and I take a step forward. I've studied grimoires at Windhaven Academy, but I've never seen one this old.

"If you are to be successful in vanquishing the soulless, you will require the assistance of the spells held within these pages," she says, running the palms of her hands over the splayed leaves.

Stepping up to it, I look from her, down to the book. The pages seem to glow from the inside out, with no other source of illumination or light being directed at the grimoire itself. Each page is worn, possibly through centuries of use. The ancient-looking texture and beautiful scrawling of the words and symbols draws me in, begging me to consume its secrets. However, none of it makes sense.

My forehead wrinkles and I bend in even closer, narrowing my gaze. "What language is this? I can't make out these words. How am I meant to use it if I can't even read it?"

I turn to her expectant gaze, and she shoots me an apologetic look. "This is written in our family's cipher. Had our training not been disrupted in your youth, you would have learned how to read and write it. I am gravely sorry this could not take place before now. But we shall have to start some training post haste, in order to make this possible."

"That all sounds well and good, but what about the stuff that's happening right now? How do I handle them?" I say, trying to be reasonable. If things are as bad as she says they are, surely getting on this is pretty important.

"Your job right now, this very moment, is to find the conjurer and gather your alliances. The soulless must be brought here as quickly as possible by you and you alone. The disruption is growing and will only become more distressing," she says. "Do not worry about the grimoire. When the time comes, you will have the enlightenment you seek. One way or another."

"Well, that's good. Because I'm pretty clueless," I say, flipping slowly through the book. There are hand-drawn images of humans, muscles, skeletal systems, plants, and so much more buried inside the pages.

"You are more awakened than you might think. Wise beyond your years, but uneducated at the same time. All of that will change," Abigail says, tipping her head in determination.

I shoot her an uneasy smile.

God, I hope she's right. This messy middle, where I'm aware there are things I'm clueless on, makes it hard to move forward with any sort of confidence.

Abigail catches my gaze. Her forehead creases as she opens and closes her mouth, evidently trying to decide on what to say. Finally, she takes a deep breath and says, "Autumn, it would do you some good to contemplate on what we do. What our kind has always tried to do. Necromancers work within the alignment of natural law, even if it appears we are bending it to our will. You would do well to remember that. Should we go beyond the bounds of those laws, there are *always* consequences to beheld."

Her words have a certain resonance and finality to them. I open my mouth to ask her what she means, when the entire catacombs begins to quake. The lighting on the walls flickers violently and I turn back to Abigail. She sets her jaw and slams the grimoire shut.

"You need to go. Now—" she demands. "Your time here is up."

CHAPTER 20

CONVERGENCE

bigail's form suddenly flickers before my eyes, jittering between solid and translucent. The rest of the space, the wall, torches, and even the floor do the same. It's as if their entire reality is threatened by whatever is making everything tremble.

Without any time to question who—*or what*—is doing it, I nod at Abigail, who returns my gaze with a deep intensity. She tips her chin and vanishes completely.

Twisting on my heel, I only manage a few steps toward the tunnel out when I'm plunged into complete darkness. I can't even make out the entrance on the other end.

Sweat beads across my forehead and my heart thrums loudly in my ears.

If I accidentally choose the wrong tunnel, missing it because I'm a step or two off, who knows where I could end up?

Closing my eyes, I inhale deeply through my nose and out through my mouth, trying to center myself. The quaking sensation tugs at the location around me, like some sort of seismic activity. Only, we're not in any kind of volcanic or earthquake zone.

Panic coils itself through my thoughts, despite trying to clear them away.

Stones crumble around me, peppering the sandy floor, and I take off running. The last thing I want is to get stuck in these catacombs if the whole thing collapses.

My vision remains dark, so I run solely on instinct, trying to make it to the other end as quickly as possible. Then, without warning, colors erupt through my perception. It starts out small at first, just little white dots at the edges of my periphery. But they get bigger, and brighter, until my entire field of vision is consumed by colors, all rotating in rapid succession. The effect is dizzying and I bend over, trying to breathe instead of hurling.

"Autumn," a voice calls in the distance. The masculine undertones of it are familiar, but I can't put my finger on why.

I perk my ears, trying to focus on the source of it.

"Autumn, come back to me...please...*please*..." It pleads. There's an edge of panic to the voice and anxiety unfurls through me like an explosion. "Come back to me. *It's not your time.*"

Suddenly, I bolt upright, finding myself in Wade's warm embrace. He lets out a cross between a sob and a sigh, pulling me against his chest.

My head swirls through thoughts, experiences, and images, but none of them stick around long enough to latch onto.

"What—what's going on?" I say, my voice sounding

distant even to me. I lick my lower lip, trying to bring moisture back to my mouth, because it feels sucked dry of every drop.

Wade refuses to let me go; instead, he clutches me so closely I can barely breathe. "I thought I'd lost you. God, Autumn, don't you ever do something like that to me again."

My eyes flicker open. The resurrection chamber's familiar energy and ambiance greet me like the comfort of a mother's embrace. Only, we're resting on the sandy floor beside the wall that leads to the catacombs.

I pull back from Wade, blinking back my surprise.

The wall is completely intact. There isn't a single stone loose or piled up on the floor.

"What the hell?" I sputter, scrambling to my feet.

Wade gropes for me. "Autumn, you should really be careful. You were—"

I stand up anyway, ignoring the dizzying sensation rolling through me. I place my hands on the stones, feeling them for any abnormality, but they're exactly as they were before I pulled them apart.

"This can't be..." I mutter, more to myself than anything.

"What is? What's going on?" Wade asks, his voice still coming out in an elevated pitch.

I point to the wall. "I went through there. This wall, it was... I..." I stutter, trying to figure out what to say or what I saw, until I remember what Abigail said. No one living should enter.

Was it all in my mind?

Wade's wide eyes show the tiniest sliver of silver and

his face is beyond pale. His complexion has taken on a greyish appearance, not unlike the revenants.

"Autumn, I thought you were dead. I don't know what's happening, but I've never been so scared in all my life," Wade breathes, his eyes pleading with me to understand the gravity of his words.

I swallow hard and take a step toward him. "I'm so sorry, Wade. I didn't mean to scare you." I pull him into my arms, wrapping them around his torso. "I didn't know."

The two of us stand there, trembling from the trauma and realization.

"I still don't understand. What were you doing? Why didn't you answer my calls?" Wade says breathlessly beside my ear. "God, as if I wasn't already having a heart attack."

"I'm sorry," I repeat, letting the guilt roll through me. "I should have. It's just—Abigail was here. She was trying to show me more about my powers. About our legacy."

Wade releases me, taking a step back. "Did she attack you?"

I chuckle softly under my breath. "No, nothing like that. She was showing me how to use a new sense of vision, I think. To see things, sense things without using my eyes. At least, that's what I thought..." My voice trails off as I try to mesh the reality of what just happened with my previous perceptions. "I thought I was in the catacombs."

Everything is suddenly thrown into question and I have the burning desire to go back in—to see if I can get back there.

"How? From here?" Wade asks, his gaze floating around the room.

I shake my head. "I'm not sure now. It all felt so real… but maybe I was just dreaming?"

"Whatever you were doing, it was not dreaming. Your body was stiff as a board and you had lost almost all color. It was like you were…" his voice quivers, but he manages to get out the last word, "*dead*."

The anguish in his face tugs at my heart, making it constrict. I step forward, placing my hands on either side of his face, staring him hard in the eyes. "You aren't getting rid of me that easily. I'm here to stay, Mr. Hoffman."

His shoulders drop and he closes his eyes. "I didn't know what to do. All I knew was I was willing to do just about anything to bring you back," he whispers.

"If it's any consolation, I think whatever you did brought me back."

Wade's dark eyebrows knit together. "What do you mean?"

I drop my hands, taking a few steps away. My eyes flit to the intact wall and I shudder away the memories of removing all of those stones. "When I was in there, everything began to shake, like there was an earthquake or something. Nothing was making sense and I was scared I wouldn't find my way out. Then…"

"Then?" he presses.

"Then there was *you*. And here I am," I say, shrugging.

Wade's face brightens at first, then falters. "We have more problems. I feel stupid even bringing it up to you after all of this, but I have to." His lips tug downward and he runs his hands through his dark hair.

My forehead creases and my heart suddenly feels like it might beat out of my chest. "What is it? What's wrong?"

He exhales a jagged breath. "I was at home when I got

a knock on the door. I thought it was you at first. I know how hard everything has been and the tension that's come between us after all of this shit...but obviously, it wasn't. It was Chelsea."

"Okay?" I say, watching as he shoves his hands into the pockets of his leather jacket. My emotions burn under the surface as I try not to jump to any conclusions.

"You know how she is—she's like a magnet for supernatural news, thanks to Sheriff Gordon," he begins.

I release a slow breath and nod. "I do."

Wade's tongue skirts across his lower lip and he says, "Well, you know the revenants we killed?"

Instantly, I know where he's going with this. "They reanimated." It wasn't a question.

Wade's eyebrows scrunch in. "How'd—?"

"Abigail," I say, raising a hand. "Go on."

He tips his chin, letting his gaze fall to the floor. Taking a moment, he blinks rapidly. "The ones they've found so far were being kept in the forensics lab at the police department. Something about weird energy signatures. But the ones we took down, they attacked the forensic scientist who was working on the case."

My hands fly to my mouth. "Oh, my god. Is the scientist okay?"

Wade nods. "Yeah, I think so. She's at the hospital, but alive, thankfully."

"Good," I say, my shoulders relaxing.

"The thing that worries me, though, is the fact that they attacked again, and they're getting stronger and more vicious. The police had to take drastic measures to take them down." Wade shudders.

"Drastic measures?" I say, quirking an eyebrow.

"They blew them up," Wade says, making a face.

I flinch.

"Chelsea said the feds are worried that the longer the revenants are up and moving, the more rabid they get. Like, they begin to operate on a whole new level of instinct. So, naturally, I wanted to warn you—and check on Grandpa. The last thing I wanted was for you to inadvertently get in the way of..." His voice drifts off and he shudders.

Realization washes through me and I feel horrible for scaring the hell out of him. "Oh, god, Wade. I should have answered—"

"Autumn, that's just it, though... My grandpa's missing."

Wade's final word hits the inside of my skull with a resounding thud.

"Are you certain? What about the boat house?"

He shakes his head. "He's gone. The door's been ripped clear off its hinges."

"Shit," I mutter. My insides feel flipped outside and I can't breathe. I wonder how long he's been gone? "If he's out—"

"He could be anywhere. And who knows what he's going to do, or who he'll attack. If the police or the feds find him—"

"They'll blow him up," I say, pacing. "If what Abigail just told me is real, I might have a way to help him. *All of them*."

Wade's gaze narrows. "What do you mean?"

"Abigail said I need to bring the bodies to the catacombs and lay them to rest. I think they'll keep coming, even if they're blown up. I don't know how, but I think they'll find a way to come back together or something. We need to end this," I say, my mind reeling.

"But how? If you only went into the catacombs inside your mind, how do we get their bodies into a metaphysical space?"

"I don't know yet, but I'll cross that bridge when we get there," I say, determination building inside my being. If there's one thing I've learned the past few months, it's that sometimes going forward takes a leap of faith, hoping the rest of the journey will appear when you need it most. "She also said I need to gather my alliances. When this happened before, it took my family, the Gilberts, and the Cranes to put an end to it. We need to take down whoever is doing this, and it's pretty obvious I can't do it alone."

"Nor should you," Wade says, his jaw setting. "But please tell me that doesn't mean what I think it means?"

"We're going to need as much help as we can get, Wade. You know this," I say, reaching out for his arm.

Wade makes a face, but nods. "Doesn't mean I have to like it."

"True," I say softly. "We also need to find someone else. Abigail was cryptic, but she said that in order to make sure no more revenants rise, we need to consecrate the cemeteries."

"How is that cryptic? Seems pretty straightforward."

"She said it has to be done by someone who has been *'touched by death, but who doesn't want to control it.'*" I say, using air quotes. "Whatever the hell that means."

Wade's eyes widen and he recoils like I just told him I'm about to grow horns.

"What is it?" I say, narrowing my gaze and reaching out for him.

He shakes his head, his hands flying to his hair, as he rakes his fingertips though the strands. "That can't be. *No...*"

"Wade?"

Suddenly, his expression brightens. "I know exactly who you're looking for."

CHAPTER 21
SWORN TO SECRECY

W ade's beautiful face is tormented as he struggles to find the words to tell me what he means. I can't help but wish I could read his mind in order to know what is making this so difficult for him.

Finally, he drops his hands to his sides and says, "Autumn, there's something I need to tell you, but I'm not sure you're gonna like it."

I blink back at him, unsure what to even say to something like that.

He swallows hard, taking a step away from me. "You were right. The day we buried my grandpa, I knew who I was talking to; it wasn't just the groundkeeper."

I stare at him, waiting for him to continue.

"I wish I could have told you then. I wish I could tell you more now, but you have to understand, we're sworn to secrecy. There are laws and if—" he swallows hard, taking a step away from me.

"What is it?" I ask. "Just say it."

He exhales, dropping his gaze to the ground. The lines on his forehead crease as he whispers, "He's my dad."

I cross my arms as an unsettling feeling washes over me. "So, your dad's not really dead?"

Wade winces, tipping his head to the side. "It's complicated."

"Wade, we're down to the wire here. Now's not the time for half-truths," I say with a little more venom than originally anticipated.

"I'm sorry, I know that. Look, there's a lot to all of this and I promise, we can get into all of it later...but for now we need to focus on the task at hand. Long story short, I think my dad is the one Abigail was referring to."

Shaking my head, I say, "What makes you think that?"

"Remember what we found in the Academy's library? It said my dad was the main suspect, right? And there were symbols on the ground," he says, his silver eyes pleading with me.

"I remember," I say, nodding.

"I don't think he was the one they were looking for. I think he was the one consecrating the cemetery," he says.

"Okay?"

Wade clears his throat. "I can't tell you why I know this yet. You'll have to trust me, Dru. I would never do anything to put you in jeopardy. As soon as I can tell you, I will."

Inhaling deeply, I tip my head in acknowledgement. "I'll hold you to it."

He nods. "Come on. First, we need to find my grandpa. My dad's not going to want to help us, so it'll give us some leverage."

I bite back more of my questions as I pull my phone

from my pocket. Dialing up Cat, I take a few steps away from him, waiting for her to pick up the line.

After a few rings, she finally answers. "Hey, Autumn. I was just thinking about—"

"Cat, I need your help," I say, cutting her off.

"What is it? What do you need?" she asks, her voice suddenly serious.

"Can you and Colton get Dominic and meet me at my house? It's important. I'll explain everything when you're here," I say, clutching the phone tightly to my ear.

Without missing a beat, she says, "On it. We'll be there in ten."

She hangs up before I can even say thank you.

Turning to Wade, I extend my arm and hold a hand out to him. "Come on. Let's see if we can find your grandpa."

He takes my hand and we make our way up the stairs. When we reach the doorway to my bedroom, twilight is descending and darkness isn't far off. A rush of adrenaline courses through my veins, and I can't help but worry about what happens when darkness falls.

Will we be able to make this all happen? How will we find the one who's been raising the dead?

There's so much that needs to happen and I don't even know if we'll be able to make it all work.

By the time we reach the front door, Dominic's car is already racing down the driveway. The loud, distinctive sports car exhaust on his Civic is hard to miss.

As I open the front door, Dominic pulls into the driveway's loop, with Cat and Colton following immediately behind in their Ford Escape.

Dominic is the first one to hop out of his vehicle. "What's up, Blackwood? Cat sounded pretty urgent.

Everything okay?" His gaze darts to Wade, then back to me.

"Let's wait for Cat and Colton," I say, tipping my chin toward their vehicle.

Colton gets out first, his dark eyes sweeping between me and Wade before his lips tug downward. Cat hops out next, practically dashing around the front of the vehicle to stand before us.

"We're here. What do you need?" Cat says, her ebony features hardening.

"Look guys, we need help finding Wade's grandpa..." I say, looking over my shoulder at Wade.

His shoulders are pulled back and his expression is as hard as the stone angel in the center of the driveway's circle.

"Wade's grandpa?" Cat says, glancing around at the other two. "I thought he was dead. Didn't you guys bury him?"

I nod. "It's a long story, but he's been brought back to life. Don't ask me how, I don't know the specifics just yet. But I'm working on it."

"Holy shit," she says, raising her hands to her mouth.

"He's been turned into a revenant—a zombie. We need to find him so we can put him to rest," I say, sweeping my gaze across the three of them.

Cat nods eagerly, Dominic shifts to one foot, looking a bit put out, but Colton turns away, shaking his head. This is the team. Wonderful.

Colton mumbles something under his breath and it sounds like, "Not gonna help him."

I roll my eyes. "Look, guys. There's more at stake here than just Wade's grandpa. There are others, too, and they need to be laid to rest. If they don't, people are going to die," I say, trying to accentuate the last word for effect. "The revenants are getting more hostile."

"That's horrible," Cat says, her eyes wide and jaw slacking open. "You're not—I mean, it wasn't you who brought these people back, was it?"

I shoot her a disgruntled look. "Of course not. Someone is trying to frame me for their resurrections. But it doesn't make them any less my responsibility. *Our* responsibility. We know about it and I've been given information on how to stop them."

The three of them exchange glances, but don't say anything.

Wade leans in and whispers in my ear. "Tell them about the last time."

Turning back to them, I nod. "This has happened before. Thirty years ago, the dead were coming back to life, and it took the efforts of all of our families. Ask your parents, if you want. But that's why I called you all here. I don't know what I'm doing, guys. I just know we're better together."

Colton snickers. "How'd you suss that one out?"

"I second that," Cat says, nodding. "I don't know anything about putting the dead to rest. That's your family's area of expertise. Now, if you want me to set 'em on fire..."

I narrow my gaze and fire back, "None of you have to understand it right now. Abigail told me what needs to be done and as far as I'm concerned, she's always been honest with me. Colton, Cat wouldn't be here if it wasn't for Abigail. I had never performed a resurrection. I didn't know what the hell I was doing." I jab a pointer finger toward Cat, who shrinks back sheepishly.

"Where do you want us to start?" Dominic says, taking a step toward us. It's the first time he's really said anything, but determination rolls off of him in waves.

Even if he doesn't like Wade, it's clear he believes me.

Relieved to have at least one of them on board, I turn to him. "Dominic, how good are your psychic abilities for locating people? Would you be able to home in on his grandpa?"

Dominic shrugs. "Your guess is as good as mine. I've never tried to locate a revenant before."

"Try. *Please*," I say, pleading with him.

He nods. "All right. But I need more to go on. Wade, do you mind?" Dominic holds out his hands, raising them up and flicking his fingertips at him.

Wade shoots me a sideways glance, but walks down the steps toward Dom.

Placing his hands on Wade's temples, Dominic closes his eyes and bows his head. Silence settles between the five of us as Dominic concentrates. Colton shakes his head, placing his hands on the back of his neck, as he walks away in disgust. Cat follows after him, grabbing onto his arm and whispering something in his ear. He stops, shooting daggers at Wade, before he nods at Cat and walks back.

"If I'm picking up on him correctly, he's nearby. Out that direction," Dominic says, dropping his hands from Wade's head and pointing out into the woods.

"There's nothing out that way but trees," Colton snickers, clearly unimpressed.

"Look, man, I know you don't wanna be here, and truth be told, I don't want you here, either. But Autumn wanted you to help, so show some damn respect," Wade says, stepping up into Colton's space.

"Guys," I warn, running up to get between the two of them. "This isn't the time or the place."

Colton glowers at us both but takes a step back.

"Who's that?" Cat says, holding her hands above her eyebrows as she squints toward the other end of the driveway.

As if on cue, we each turn to follow her gaze. A black SUV comes barreling down the driveway with the headlights flashing brightly as it hits the various dips in the drive.

"I have no idea," I say, shaking my head and watching, mesmerized, as the newcomers circle up to us.

I've never seen the vehicle before in my life. The windows are tinted to the point of being completely blacked out and I narrow my gaze, trying to make out who could be inside.

The passenger door opens up first, and out steps the international psychic, Diana. Her bright pink hair flaps haphazardly in the breeze and in this low light, she looks like she could be Dominic's younger sister.

"Hey there, kiddos. Miss me?" she says, eyeing me and Wade. She shoots us both a genuine smile.

I glance over at Wade, who shrugs in return.

Colton and Cat exchange confused looks, but keep their mouth shut.

"Who's—?" Dominic begins, but promptly clamps his mouth shut when the driver's side door opens.

A guy in his mid-forties with black hair and a similar sense of style to Wade walks around the vehicle. His dark, discerning eyes scan each of us before landing back with Diana. Without a word, she nods at him.

The man's lips press into a thin line and he tips his chin.

Then, he walks up to me, looks me straight in the eye, and says, "Autumn Blackwood, you're under arrest for suspicion of criminal resurrection."

CHAPTER 22
UNLEASHING PANDORA

My mind is a whirling cyclone of jumbled thoughts as the federal agent pulls my arms around my back. His hands are surprisingly smooth as he places cuffs around my wrists. The cold metal, however, digs into my skin, putting things into sharp contrast.

"Arrest? She didn't do anything wrong," I hear Wade sputter, but his words are so far away. It's like they're completely separated from reality.

Arrest...

As we move toward the SUV, everything moves in slow motion. It's as if I've managed to slow down everyone else while I'm moving super-quick. Only, I know better.

Instead, I'm trying desperately to cling to the moment because my future has just come crashing down around me.

I can't go to prison. I can't go to prison.

No matter how hard I try, I can't seem to focus on anyone or anything. It isn't until my eyes land on Diana and a broad, goofy grin spreads across her face that I come crashing back to Earth. Her smile snaps everything back into focus as a deep pool of anger flares through my veins.

Just as I open my mouth to give her a piece of my mind, she winks at me. Like, actually winks. The gesture is so out of place in this situation, and while she doesn't pull it off in the same suavity as Wade, it pulls me up short.

"Wait—" Colton says, stepping forward and holding his hands out in front of him. He takes a deep breath and exhales it slowly. "*Wait*."

The agent stops moving us toward the black vehicle. "Step aside, kid."

Colton shakes his head, getting between me and the vehicle. His eyes are wide and he shakes his head frantically. "No, you've gotta listen to me. It's not her. You have the wrong person."

"That's ridiculous. All the evidence is pointing directly at her," the federal agent says.

My heart catches in my throat and I hang my head in defeat.

"I have a hunch you should hear him out, Blake," Diana says, smirking as she crosses her arms over her torso.

Blake doesn't even bat an eye. As if there's not even a question to her hunches, he turns back to Colton. "I'm listening."

Colton runs his hand over his mouth, his dark-brown eyes pleading with me, but I don't know what we're bargaining for.

"What's going on here?" Cat asks, her face full of concern as she steps up to Colton and reaches for his arm.

Colton swallows hard, glancing from her back to Blake.

"It was me. I was the one who was summoning them. All of them."

My mouth pops open.

"What?" Wade growls behind me. "All this time—it was you?"

Colton flicks his gaze to Wade, but ignores the comment. Instead, choosing to focus on the federal agent. "It started out harmless—really. All I wanted to do was get rid of..." his lips tighten and he stares at the ground. "I thought if I made it look like he was bad news, Autumn would break up with him."

My anger bursts into flames. "It was you? The anonymous text? The video that went viral around the school? What in the hell, Colton?"

"I know—I never meant for you to get involved, Autumn. It was just supposed to be him. If I had known..." he says, his voice drifting off.

"I can't believe this," Wade says, taking a step back and running his hands through his hair. "You were trying to ruin my life—my reputation and *relationship*. Make me leave Windhaven. Who the hell do you think you are?"

"You don't deserve her," Colton spits, his face contorting with anguish. "She deserves better—she deserves..."

"You?" Wade snickers. "Come on, man. You think this is better? Or that this is what she wants...or what would impress her?" Wade moves toward Colton with clenched fists. "You clearly have no idea who Autumn really is."

"Eh—that's close enough, lover boy," Diana says, holding her hands out and stopping Wade's forward momentum. Her chin tips downward, making her pink hair ruffle in the cool breeze.

"But you heard him—" Wade says, through clenched teeth.

"I did. And so did everyone else here," Diana says, pointedly.

Colton throws daggers at Wade with his eyes. "Whatever, man. You shouldn't even be here. Dominic's told me about you. Your kind shouldn't even be anywhere *near* her."

Dom's eyes pop open and he raises his hands. "Hey now, don't bring me into this."

Wade takes a step back, rolling his eyes. "Again with the *my kind* bullshit."

"But it's true," Colton says, frowning as he faces Dominic. "You said he's forbidden—that he shouldn't be anywhere near her, and if he was outta the picture, I'd have a chance with Autumn."

"Yeah, but I didn't mean this way," Dominic says, shaking his head.

Colton eyes are glassed over and his words come out choked. "But what about the kiss?"

Wade's head whips toward me. "Kiss?" The level of heartbreak evident in his eyes makes my soul ache.

Dammit—I should have told him sooner.

I shake my head. "It wasn't—it's not like that."

Colton's eyes narrow. "It's exactly like that. We kissed, Autumn. You can't erase that, even if you think you want to."

"*You* kissed me, Colton," I fire back. "I didn't ask for it —and I certainly didn't expect it."

"But…" Colton says, his eyebrows tipping up in the middle.

"Wait—what?" Cat says, gawking. "When did this happen? How did I not know about it?"

"Looks like Autumn's been keeping it from everyone," Wade mutters, taking a step back.

Holding Wade's gaze, I try to will to him my thoughts and feelings, but it's no use. I can see him slipping away from me right before my eyes.

I look over to Cat, trying to ignore the thrumming of my heartbeat against my chest. "It was nothing. I'd written it off as a momentary lapse of reason. It's why I didn't tell you, Wade. It was *nothing*."

Wade's face is drained of all color and he looks as though he might be sick.

"When? Where was I?" Cat demands.

"It was after your accident. We had just gotten you back," I say, exhaling all of my pent-up energy. I want to reach for Wade, to comfort him, but I can't do anything with my damn hands behind my back. "I thought he was just relieved—and it was an accident. I didn't think he really meant anything by it."

"So, while my grandpa died, and his sister nearly did, he was making the moves on you?" Wade says, shaking his head and turning toward the house. "Unreal."

"It didn't mean anything," I repeat warily.

Colton's expression is a mangled mess of agony. "But I thought..." he mumbles.

"So, if I'm getting this right, Colton, you're confessing to the summoning of the revenants?" Blake says, reaching for his handcuff keys.

Colton's dark eyes dart to Blake, defeated. "Yes."

"Is this at both the Windhaven and Mistwood Point cemeteries?" Blake continues.

"Yes."

"All right." Blake unlocks the cuffs, releasing my hands and walking over to Colton. "Mr. Gilbert, you're under arrest for criminal resurrection. You'll need to come with us."

Colton nods his head, turning around and bringing his arms behind his back so Blake can put the cuffs on him.

"But—this doesn't make any sense," I say, shaking my head. "Colton, you're an elemental witch. You can bend earth to your will. How could you summon people? I thought—?"

"As luck would have it, elemental witches who get their power from earth energies can resurrect bodies," Diana says, eyeing her nails like they're the most interesting thing about this afternoon. "But Gemini Twins—see, their power grows exponentially when they feel threatened." She turns her discerning gaze to Cat and quirks an eyebrow.

"You knew, didn't you? My arrest was all just a ruse," I say, shaking my head. The adrenaline rush is starting to wear off and I can't believe anything I'm hearing. It's like I've stepped into an alternate universe.

Diana shifts her gaze to me and smiles sweetly. "I wouldn't be world-renowned if I didn't figure it out. Besides, I promised I'd take care of you, didn't I?"

I raise my eyebrows in agreement. Part of me is flooding with relief...but the other half is hurting for Colton. He's not a bad guy—far from it. But his feelings clouded his judgment.

"What's going to happen to him?" I ask, suddenly scared for him.

Diana tips her head. "That'll be up to him."

Blake steps around Colton, so he can open the back door to the SUV. "If he cooperates, we might be able to get his sentence lightened. So, I hope you're ready. You're gonna need to help us undo this mess, kid. "

Colton nods, refusing to look up to any of us.

"The spellwork isn't going to be any fun, that's for sure," Diana mutters, practically prancing over to the vehicle.

Colton's eyes widen as he glances to Diana, but he doesn't say anything. What was the spell like to raise the dead in the first place? Was it like the resurrection I performed on Cat?

Blake points to the seat and Colton promptly sits down.

As Colton's door clicks into place, Cat springs into action. "Hold on. I'm coming with you. I'm not letting him go alone."

Before any of us knows it, she's hopped into the back seat alongside her brother.

Diana nods, as if totally expecting her outburst. She looks to each one of us before saying, "Well, it's been a blast, but it looks like we all have our work cut out for us. See ya around, kids. Good luck. I trust you'll be able to get this next step done."

With that, she hops into the passenger side and closes the door. The black SUV speeds off, leaving Wade, Dominic, and me in a stupor.

Rubbing at my left wrist, I turn to Wade. His expression is distant as he eyes me wearily.

Taking a deep breath, I say, "Wade, I know you're probably..."

He cuts me off, raising a hand. His jaw clenches and his

voice is tight. "Not now, Autumn. It's not the time. We still need to find my grandpa."

I blink back my regret and bite my lip to keep it from quivering.

What have I done?

Dominic's eyebrows raise and he steps forward, taking the lead. "Alrighty—on that note...let's get moving. It's almost dark. Like I said, he's out that way, but I don't know for how long."

I nod, unable to form any words that could relieve the tension that's settled between my heart and stomach. Instead, I look over my shoulder as the SUV vanishes from sight.

How did I not see what was happening with Colton? Had I just realized how deep his feelings were, maybe I could have prevented all of this... Was I just too wrapped up in my feelings for Wade to see the truth? Or worse... was I too afraid to face Colton's feelings because I already knew? It's not like the kiss hasn't been weighing heavily on my mind since it happened. Yet, I chose to ignore it and try to let it slide so I could pretend like it never happened.

A horrible truth erupts in the pit of my stomach. Not only have I let Wade down...I let down Colton, too. Had I been honest from the beginning, none of this would have happened.

This is all my fault.

CHAPTER 23

A DEATH WISH

"So, not to be a complete moron or anything—but have you thought about how you're going to restrain gramps once we find him?" Dominic asks, flipping on the flashlight from his phone.

I shoot Wade a sideways glance and he shrugs. "Guess we'll deal with that once we get there."

"Reassuring," Dominic mutters, stepping out in front and taking the lead.

Cringing internally, I'm right there with Dominic. The last time we were near Wade's grandpa, he was pretty spry for a dead guy. And damn scary.

"We handled him just fine last time. I'm sure we'll be able to handle him this time," Wade says nonchalantly as he shoves his hands in his pockets. "Besides, he's outnumbered three to one."

"Didn't know there was a rule on the number of people it takes to wrangle a dead guy," Dom mutters.

The sunlight has all but dwindled and the March evening chill has settled in. Pulling my coat in tighter, I shudder against its bite. My toes are already aching from the cold.

Unable to calm my mind, I let my thoughts tumble around like they've been put into one of those gemstone tumblers and it's been left on too long. I can't help but worry about Colton and what's going to happen to him now. But I'm also apprehensive about what we're up against.

One piece of the puzzle has fit into place—we know who's been behind the attacks. But what had Abigail said? We still need to get all the bodies into the catacombs and consecrate the cemeteries to stop them from continuing to rise. It feels like a huge expanse we're trying to cover, and I feel totally unequipped to be able to handle it. I must not be the only one, either. Both of the guys continue walking without much in the way of discussion.

"How much farther?" Wade finally asks, pulling his collar up to protect his neck.

Dominic points ahead of us. "See that hill over there? What's back there?"

I peer over his shoulder, trying to get a better look. From here, the only thing I get the sense of is how creepy the trees look in the light of his phone. It reminds me of *The Blair Witch Project*. I'd rather be doing anything else.

"I don't see anything..." I say, moving forward with even less enthusiasm.

"Yeah, me either. But I keep getting the impression he's out that way," Dominic says.

"Isn't this where we were looking the other day?" Wade asks, speaking his first words directly to me in the past half hour.

My heart lightens and I nod. "Yeah, but we're a bit farther now. I don't think we made it quite this far."

The memory of that day rushes at me like a freight train. It had been a good day—a sexy, kinda romantic day. Well, until grandpa showed up, anyway.

I shudder away the remnants of that day and breathe out my trepidation. This might not be how I'd wanted things to play out, but hopefully it will all be over soon. At least the truth is out there now, and I don't have to carry the burden of it anymore. When this revenant thing is done and dusted, hopefully Wade and I can work everything out.

Please, let us work this out...

Unfortunately, a niggling feeling in the back of my mind makes me uneasy. Colton mentioned Wade wasn't allowed to be with me, and Dominic said something to that effect last year. It seems like everyone knows more about what Wade is than I do.

My gaze drifts over to him and again, a twinge of guilt and anxiety blossom through me. His dark hair flutters in the breeze and he keeps his eyes trained only on the path ahead. He hasn't even tried to hold my hand once. I drop my chin and tuck my hands in my coat pockets.

For the next few minutes, only the sound of our feet crunching in the snow breaks the silence. Then, in the distance, an owl hoots, making me nearly jump out of my skin.

Dominic chuckles under his breath. "Kinda jumpy for someone who raises the dead, aren't ya?"

I scratch at the side of my temple and make a face. "Yeah, well, I'm not exactly used to it yet. And I'm not overly looking forward to any of this, so..."

"Shhh... Do you hear that?" Wade says, holding up a hand and cocking his head to the side.

At first, I don't hear a thing, but after a few seconds of holding my breath, a faint thumping echoes across the snowy landscape.

My eyes widen. "What is that? Do you think it's your grandpa?"

Wade shrugs. "Hell if I know. I can't say he normally made a sound like that."

I shrink back, feeling stupid.

"We'll know soon enough. If my abilities aren't completely off base, he should be right over this crest. You ready?" Dominic says, lowering his voice.

"As ready as we'll ever be, I suppose," I say, shrugging. It's not as if I want to stand outside all night. In fact, I'd rather hurry this up so I can talk to Wade.

Together, we make our way the remaining few feet up a small hill, holding onto barren trees for support so we don't slip back down. The ground beneath our feet is disheveled and slick, as if someone—or something—has been here in the not-too-distant past.

When we reach the top, down on the other side is an enormous oak tree bigger than any tree I've ever seen before. Its trunk had been mostly obscured by the hill, showing off only its branches. However, its wide base spans at least five feet in diameter, probably more. Those large, gnarly branches claw upward, breaking off into hundreds, maybe thousands, of smaller branches.

Just beside the tree, as if it were built as a support, is a small stone entrance. It's barely noticeable, but scattered on the ground are large icicles and a smattering of snow. When the icicles were intact, they would have easily hidden the entrance to the casual observer. I know I would never have thought twice had I seen it. Hell, in the summer, it's probably equally hidden by all of the brush.

The dark mouth is no wider than two feet across and roughly five feet tall. But it's just about the right size for a person...

Dominic casts a leery grin my direction, then shines the flashlight at Wade. "Well, it's your grandpa. *You* go first."

Wade scowls, dropping his arms to his sides and stepping in front to take the lead. I follow him, refusing to allow the panic welling up inside of me to win. We did deal with him before and I'll be damned if I make Wade handle things alone.

As we get to the entrance, Wade pulls out his own phone and turns on the flashlight. Glancing over his shoulder, he says, "Stay behind me. If he runs at us like he did last time—just go. I've got this."

My mouth drops open. "Got this? In what universe do you have this?"

Why doesn't he want me here? Does he have a death wish now?

Instead of answering me, he turns back around, facing the way of the tunnel. Our curiosity doesn't take long to catch up with us. The tunnel is barely longer than a room's length—maybe ten or twelve feet. It's made out of the same stone and mortar work as the resurrection chamber in my house...only at the other end is a large, ancient-looking wooden door. Ornate black iron details are strewn across its surface like some sort of incantation. And maybe it is.

Right in the middle of the door, bumping into it over and over again, is Wade's grandpa.

"Is that—?" Dom whispers behind me.

I nod, refusing to take my eyes off him for fear he'll turn around and run this way. Wade and I know first-hand how fast he can move and how strong he is.

Reaching for Wade's shoulder, I lean in. His scent of sandalwood and soap tickle my senses and twist my guilt. Shoving it back down, I say, "What's he doing?"

Wade shakes his head and shrugs. "I don't know... I'm still new to revenants. It looks like he's trying to get in, though."

"What is this place? How did it get here?" Dominic whispers feverishly. "I can't get a single read on it. It's like a black hole to my ability. Is this part of your property still?"

"I'm not sure," I say, running my fingertips over my mouth. "I've never seen it before—but..."

"It's gotta be the entrance to the catacombs," Wade says, finishing my thought.

I nod in agreement.

Dominic's eyes practically fall out of his head. "The what now?"

"It's a long story. I'll fill you in later. All you need to know is this is the perfect place for him to be. It actually helps me out a lot because I need to get him inside," I say, stepping around Wade as I try to get a better view of the door.

The handle isn't evident, nor is any kind of a lock. Instead, the massive gateway looks impenetrable. I need to figure out how to open the door, and hopefully I'll be able to convince Grandpa to follow me—or at least go inside of his own volition. Maybe once Colton does his side of things, Grandpa will be totally compliant until he's been released to the catacombs.

"You wanna get that guy in there? That's a special kinda crazy," Dominic whispers. "I wouldn't go anywhere near that place. Bad mojo..."

"Thanks," I mutter, making a face.

"Well, we can't just stand here and stare at him all day. If that's the door to the catacombs, we need to get it open and get him inside." Wade walks forward, his arm outstretched.

Reaching for him, I yank him back. "No, you can't go in there. I'm not even sure you should touch the door."

"What? Why?" Wade says, his eyebrows pulling in.

"Your job has to be finding out how to consecrate the cemeteries. Remember?" I say, trying to calm the thumping of my heart.

"I'm kinda with Wade on this one. Why can't we help with this first?" Dominic asks, tipping his chin toward the doorway.

"Because only the dead shall enter," I say, frowning.

Dominic snickers. "You're not dead."

"I know that," I say, shooting him a look of irritation. "But my family is an exception."

"Lucky," he says, quirking an eyebrow sarcastically.

"Look, I didn't make the rules. I just know that if either of you try to enter the catacombs, your souls could be lost. It's a magical labyrinth in there—and if your soul isn't being properly guided, you could get trapped in Purgatory. So, trust me, you don't wanna open that door, okay?" I turn to Wade, whose expression is quizzical, but he doesn't say a word.

Suddenly, Wade's grandpa stops thumping against the door. The silence immediately fills the space and pushes a shot of adrenaline through my system. Wade crouches, taking a stance I've only ever seen football players make, while Dom doesn't move a muscle. Twisting around on the spot, Wade's grandpa flits his hazy white eyes over the three of us and releases the most horrifying high-pitched scream.

Dominic's mouth opens, his own scream mingling with the sound of the revenant's. I open my mouth at the same time, but no sound escapes, no matter how hard I try.

Wade, on the other hand, looks up to the ceiling of the small interior space and yells, "Dad—"

CHAPTER 24
A GUARANTEE

Black smoke billows behind us, consuming the opening of the tunnel as it sends dark tendrils out in every direction. Like the darkness of a black hole, no light comes in or out when both Wade and Dominic shine their flashlights into it.

Then, materializing out of the darkness, is the man I've seen twice now. The pure panic and fear in the tone of Wade's voice must have been enough to summon his father—whatever he is. His silver eyes survey the scene with deep discernment, and apprehension is painted across his features. When his eyes pause on the revenant behind Wade, his jaw clenches and eyebrows lower. When Wade's dad raises a single hand, the revenant's cry ceases, and he drops into a strange, silent trance.

"What's going on here?" Wade's dad says, his voice a pile of gravel as he turns to Wade. The darkness that brought him here vanishes as if sucked through a vortex in his back.

Wade takes a deep breath, straightening his shoulders

as he walks toward him. "Things have worsened, as you can probably see. I know you said not to," He starts to turn around, pointing toward the revenant of his grandpa.

"And yet, here we are," his dad says, blinking slowly and flitting his gaze to me long enough to send a wave of anxiety rolling through me.

I swallow hard, trying to muster the courage to be more confident than I feel. "Someone has been raising the dead. We know you were a suspect the last time this happened, but it wasn't you."

For the first time, a hint of surprise flashes across his dad's features. "And how would you know this?" His eyes land squarely on Wade, who drops his gaze to the ground and shakes his head imperceptibly.

I narrow my eyes and jut out my jaw. "Look, I don't know what you did back then or why, but we need your help now to consecrate the cemeteries involved. Wade believes this is something you can do." Squirming under the weight of his stare, I add, "Is...is it something you can do?"

Wade's dad is far more commanding of the space than any of us. Even Dominic shrinks back as Wade's dad steps toward me. "I told you I would be back. It appears your meddling has caught up with you, has it?"

I shake my head vehemently. "This wasn't me."

His eyes narrow down to silver slits, but he tips his head to the side. "Surprising. This has the stench of your family's tampering all over it."

I practically snort. "Stench of my family's tampering? Excuse me? What is your problem?"

Wade steps between me and his dad, splaying his arms

out wide in protection. I peer over his shoulder, refusing to cower. No matter who this guy thinks he is.

Wade takes a tentative step forward. "It wasn't her. The guy who did it is in custody and is working to reverse the spell. But Autumn's right. We need your help to consecrate the graves so the cemetery returns to its tranquility. All things considered, I know I can't—"

Wade's dad raises a hand, cutting him off. "If you are asking to change my mind..."

"No—nothing's changed. I just mean, I know I can't, but you can. Autumn is doing everything she can to put things right and she's only got half of the pieces. Please, just help us," Wade says, dropping his arms by his side.

"The revenants cannot return to the cemeteries..." Wade's dad begins.

Wade nods. "We know. Autumn is going to lay them to rest inside."

As if this makes total sense, he drops his chin in apparent understanding. "Fine. So long as his remains are taken within, I will do as you wish. But this doesn't change anything—"

Wade nods feverishly. "I know. I get it."

"I'm glad someone does, because this conversation is cryptic at best," Dom mutters under his breath. "Even for me."

"Fine," he nods.

Wade exhales slowly, letting his shoulders drop. "Thank you."

"Which cemeteries have been desecrated by this magic?" His dad asks, flashing his eyes to me again.

"Windhaven and Mistwood Point. They'll—"

Before Wade can get any other words out, his dad

opens the smokey black portal and turns to walk through it. However, he stops, turning back to us. "You'll need this, necromancer."

From what appeared to be an empty hand, he flicks his wrist like he's throwing a frisbee—but what extends from his grasp is more like a bright yellow cord of light. It winds its way around grandpa's revenant, binding him around the midsection. The other end bonds itself to my midsection in much the same way.

"What is this?" I say, raising my arms in surprise.

"A guarantee. You're bound together now. Until put to rest, you can't lose him. That's not a problem, is it?" he says, raising a single, sardonic eyebrow.

"N-no...but how do I get rid of it?" I ask, poking the energetic rope with my pointer finger. The energy of it feels like swiping your finger through a running kitchen tap. And just like the water, it remains intact even as my finger moves through it.

"You won't have to. As soon as his body is released, so will the cord." With that, Wade's dad walks straight into the black portal and vanishes as it condenses in on itself.

"Well, on the upside, it looks like whatever your dad did calmed it down," Dominic says, raising his eyebrows to his hairline.

"All right, so what do we do to help?" Wade says, ignoring Dominic and turning to me.

I shake my head. "Other than helping to round up the other revenants, nothing beyond this point. I have to do this alone."

"Are you sure we can't—" Wade begins.

"I'm sure," I nod.

"Well, I, for one, wouldn't enter in there if someone

paid me. It's like whatever's on the other side of that door doesn't even exist," Dominic says, shuddering.

"Go see Sheriff Gordon and find a way to round up the others. Bring them here," I say, turning to the door. "I'm going to find Abigail and get started."

Wade nods. "All right, we can do that." He takes a few steps toward the entrance but stops and turns back to me. "Be careful. Please." His eyes plead with me and my solar plexus constricts.

Holding his gaze, I place a hand on his cheek. "I will. Make sure you do the same. Okay?"

His lips press into a thin line, but he dips his chin.

"Text me when you're back and I'll come to collect them, but do not, under any circumstances, come inside. Either of you," I say, eyeing them both.

Again, Wade nods. Turning to Dominic, he says, "Come on."

Casting one quick glance as his grandpa's still body, Wade walks out, back the way we came in.

"See ya around. Try not to be zombie food, okay?" Dominic says, slapping me on the shoulder as he walks out after Wade.

"They're *revenants*," I say, sticking a tongue out.

"Tomato, tomahto," he says over his shoulder.

Grinning to myself, I shake my head and turn to face the door. Grandpa continues to hover beside me, as if in some sort of status, but for my own peace of mind, I don't want to linger long.

"All right, Autumn, let's figure this thing out..." I mutter to myself as I walk up to the wooden door.

As it turns out, the doorway isn't as unusual as originally thought. Instead, it's two halves to one whole, with enormous twin iron handles arching on either side of the door's middle split. When Wade's grandpa was in the way, he just blocked their view.

Taking a deep breath, I grab the right handle and pull. The door groans but doesn't budge. Panic unfurls in my mind as I drop the handle and pull up short. However, the more I look at the door's architecture, I realize how much of an idiot I am.

Putting the palms of my hands on the wood, I press hard, instead. This time, the wood creaks open, allowing a draft of cool air to scurry out. Beyond the entrance, the inner tunnel is as black as the portal Wade's dad emerged from.

What if this isn't the entrance to the catacombs? What if I get lost?

The thought interrupts my forward momentum, unleashing a torrent of panic. I have no idea what I'm doing...and no idea if I'm even in the right place. What if I'm wrong? What if everything I saw inside the catacombs wasn't even real?

What if it is, but I'm not deemed worthy this time? Could I be lost in here forever?

Before I have more time to second-guess myself, torches, similar to the ones inside the resurrection chamber back in the house, begin to ignite along the tunnel walls. I can't see anything beyond them, but a sudden urgency beckons me. A warm, calming sensation sweeps through my body and I can't help but take a step forward.

I cross the threshold of the catacombs, entering the sacred space. The sensation is like stepping through a curtain of water and emerging on the other side. The energy brushes past my cheeks, tickling my senses, and heightening every ability. Whatever magic protects this space from Dominic's abilities seems to have accepted me as one of its own.

The pathway to where I need to go emerges in my mind, like a holographic Google map only I can see. No longer scared about where to go or how to get there, I follow my instincts and the direction being unveiled for me.

The deeper we go, a strong fragrance of frankincense greets us. At first, it's just a hint, but quickly overpowers any of the earthy scents trying to permeate the space. With each step forward, more torches ignite while others go out. Occasionally, there are paths that lead off from the main tunnel and sometimes torches even light up, as if tempting me to venture off from the path. However, my internal compass continues to guide me and I follow its calling, ignoring all others.

We walk for a good fifteen minutes, taking a number of turns. While I know I'm on the right path here beneath the ground, I've lost all direction to where my house is on the property. My only hope is that my experience with Abigail earlier won't fail me.

As I take a final left turn, Wade's grandpa and I leave the darkness of the tunnels and emerge into the large circular room I had seen in my vision. Walking into the space, Abigail awaits, hovering just off to the side with an expectant smile on her face. In the center of the room, the grimoire rests on the pedestal as if awaiting my summons.

"Abigail, it's time. I need to know how to put the revenants to rest," I say, looking over my shoulder at Wade's grandpa, who has mimicked my halt.

She nods, eyeing Wade's grandpa as she points to the grimoire. "The spell is not difficult, but it requires your utmost attention. You must bless the soulless and inter them so their bodies may finally be at rest. Should your attention slip, even but a little, it would be most dreadful."

I walk over to the book with grandpa in tow. Looking over the open pages, the anxiety I felt before blossoms again inside my stomach. I still can't read the pages...

"What do I need to do?" I ask.

"Are all of them within the catacombs?" Abigail asks, her eyebrows furrowing.

I shake my head. "No, not yet. We're working on it. They'll be here soon."

Abigail's expression cools, but she tips her head in acknowledgement. "Let us try on this one first. I will walk you through the words and help you with their saying. You shall find once the words are spoken out loud, they will become a part of you, making each interment easier."

"That sounds good," I say, letting my shoulders relax and my gaze fall back to the book.

"Sorry, but I can't let you do that," a woman's voice hisses from the shadows.

CHAPTER 25
FETCH

My head jerks up and my eyes search wildly for the source of the words. Without feeling the need to stay hidden, Cat slinks from the shadows, crossing her arms behind her back.

"Be cautious," Abigail warns, moving closer to me.

I narrow my gaze, shaking my head. "How...?"

For some reason, my brain doesn't seem to want to make sense of seeing her here. Alarm bells ring like they're announcing Armageddon, but the best I can do is gawk at her.

A sly grin spreads across Cat's lips, and she takes another step closer. "It is a bit miraculous, isn't it? I never in a million years thought I'd find my way through this maze. Fate has a funny way of delivering, doesn't it?"

Confusion swirls around inside my brain like a caged bird and I can't help but wonder what in the world is going on. The last time I saw Cat, she was leaving with Colton. I highly doubt she'd leave his side unless—

My mouth drops open. "Was there an accident? Omg...

you're not..." I take a step toward her, my heart thudding haphazardly in my chest. I can't bring myself to say the final word, just in case it could be true.

Abigail moves quickly, coming between me and Cat. "Guard the revenant," she says as she passes me. "Be gone, foul thing. You are an unholy abomination and not welcome in this sacred space."

"I'm hurt, truly," Cat says, pressing her right hand to her heart and taking another measured step inside the room.

"Abigail," I sputter, unable to make sense of anything going on here. "This is my *friend*—you helped me *save* her."

Glancing over her shoulder, Abigail shakes her head. "This is but an echo of your friend, a remnant of her soul which needs to be reclaimed. Surely you can feel it?"

My eyes widen as I peer from her to Cat.

This isn't Cat? The *real* Cat?

Suddenly, all of the odd exchanges I've had with her over the past few months come into focus. Things have felt off from time to time—but I couldn't put my finger on why. Not to mention when Wade and I saw her on the side of the road...

"What is she?" I say, taking a step back and forcing Wade's grandpa to shuffle behind me.

"A Fetch," Abigail says, keeping her eyes trained ahead of her. Without looking behind her, she raises a finger and points to the grimoire. "It is of utmost importance that you continue your work. Quickly."

"But I can't read it—" I say, fumbling my way back to the book. "And what the hell is a Fetch?"

"See, this is a predicament we're in here, ladies. An impasse, actually. I've been working very hard to destabilize things and I can't have you putting it all back the way it was before," Cat's doppelgänger says, her voice painted with thinly veiled fury. "I want *more*."

"The Fetch must have come into being at the time of Ms. Gilbert's resurrection. It has been known to happen, though I know not why it would have done so for her," Abigail says, refusing to divert her gaze from Cat. "I know not how, but I believe she is syphoning the power used to bring these revenants to life. It must be merged into the remainder of your friend's soul, but this level of magic will take its toll."

"Oh, no...there will be no merging; no resting. No releasing my pets. I have been buried in the shadows of that Goodie Two-shoes for far too long. I refuse to go back to the way things were. I have far too much to do," Cat says, casually stepping forward, her hands still behind her back.

My pulse races and a cold sweat breaks out across my forehead.

She's toying with us... But why? What is it she thinks she'll get from us here?

Glancing down at the grimoire, the power and energy of it radiates into the palms of my hands. Centuries of magic have been imbued into these pages, and while I may not yet understand the contents, I don't have to be told that having it fall into the wrong hands could be catastrophic. Why else would it be hidden here?

"What do you need me to do?" I say, flipping through the pages quickly.

Abigail shakes her head. "You do not yet possess the power to accomplish what needs to be done. It shall have to be me..."

Without waiting for Cat to make a move, Abigail raises her arms out wide, chanting something just under her breath. The torches on the walls flicker, and deep beneath our feet, the catacombs rumble with a power I've never experienced. It puts every cell in my body on notice, and I know Cat feels it, too. While she might not be corporeal, Abigail's etheric energy is still a force to reckon with.

Cat screeches, bounding forward at Abigail, but stumbles as she goes straight through her ghostly body. I cry out in alarm, slamming the grimoire shut and pulling it to my chest to protect it. There is no way I'm letting the Fetch get ahold of this book. No matter how much she looks like my best friend.

"You know, your dead grandma isn't as daft as she appears," she says, picking herself up off the floor and dusting at her arms. "When I gave Colton the idea to raise the dead, I didn't know it would lead me here so soon. As my plan took form, I thought for sure it would take ages to find out where the Blackwood grimoire was hidden."

"You're not going to get it," I say, taking another step backward.

Abigail continues to summon whatever magic is needed, but so far it's not enough to stop the Fetch's advancements. She continues to walk toward me like a true cat stalking its prey.

"It doesn't have to be this way," Cat purrs. "We could work together in this. Imagine the ways we could bend the laws of life to our will."

I look over at Wade's grandpa; his ashen form continues to hover just off to my left, waiting in his strange stand-by mode for whatever his next mission will be. Why would anyone want to bend life and death to their own whim? Who would ever want that kind of burden?

Sometimes, the dead should stay that way.

"I don't get it... the Gilbert family should have its own grimoire. Why not leech from that one? You come from a powerful family," I say, trying to buy Abigail more time.

"True," Cat nods. She keeps her gaze on me, evidently unfazed by whatever Abigail is doing, Instead, she puts her entire focus on making her way to me. "But their book is nowhere near as powerful as I need. They don't possess any of the ancient secrets to life and death. That's why you're going to hand over yours."

"Over my dead body," I mutter through clenched teeth. Energy begins to radiate in the palms of my hands, making them burn where I clutch the ancient tome.

Cat's doppelgänger smiles. "That can be arranged."

"Do not listen to her. If she had such power, she would not be tormenting us so," Abigail says, turning to face us. Her eyes have abandoned their soft-green color for a sheath of pure white.

The room begins to radiate—glowing with a white light that expands outward from the center of Abigail. Suddenly, it condenses to a beam that seeks out Cat like a spotlight hunting for a prisoner trying to escape.

When the light hits her, she drops to her knees, crying out in pain. The light consumes her, then bounces off, refracting though the ceiling as if seeking out another source. However, as quickly as it was lit, the light pulls back, practically knocking Abigail to the ground.

Cat's screeches subside as the light peters out. Raising her chin from her chest, her dark eyes meet mine as her lips curve into a wicked grin.

"Whoopsie. Looks like that didn't work," she says, as if she knew full well whatever Abigail was doing would be fruitless.

"How—?" Abigail says wearily as she drops to the ground.

"Silly old fool. You don't have anywhere near the capability to mess with the souls of Gemini Twins. The only one who has that kind of power is God—and maybe Death if he feels particularly generous. Good luck getting either of them on your side right now," Cat says, chuckling.

"Gemini Twin," Abigail mutters, raising a hand to her head. Her body flickers in and out of focus, shifting like a TV station receiving too much static. Then, with a simple blink, she vanishes.

Without Abigail's knowledge and power and direction, I feel completely exposed. If Abigail's abilities weren't enough, none of mine stand a chance against whatever a Gemini Twin is, either.

Unable to think of any other way to protect the grimoire, I take off running. I turn down the first tunnel, racing into the darkness. Wade's grandpa follows me, his energetic cord continuing to hold as I try to make an escape. Behind me, the Fetch's footsteps aren't far behind. I keep running, hoping my eyes will adjust to the darkness or the torches will light, but when they don't I fumble for my phone.

It drops from my hand, landing on the soft dirt with a thud.

"Dammit," I say, panting. Panic erupts through my gut, launching a dose of adrenaline, and I keep running, unable to justify slowing down to grab it.

If I'm going to get away from the Fetch, I'll need to lose her in these tunnels. But how...?

Suddenly, I close my eyes, trying to summon the sight Abigail had shown me earlier. I have no idea if it is a trick my astral self can use while my real self can't...but there's no time like the present to try.

Please, please, please work.

I continue to run, hoping my other senses will alert me if I'm about to faceplant into a wall or something.

"There's no point in running, Autumn. I'll find you," the Fetch calls after me. Her voice echoes through the chamber halls, sending chills up my spine.

Then, as if a theater screen ignites in my mind, the spectrum of colors erupts, showing me the faint outlines of the tunnel walls and its offshoots. The walls are full of small archways, one on top of the other above a flat plat-form. Inside each archway are the bodies of hundreds, if not thousands, of people who have sought sanctuary in these catacombs. The realization makes me shudder, but I keep running, taking turn after turn in the hopes of losing her.

Taking an immediate left, I veer the revenant and I as far away from where we started as possible. It's only after the first twenty or so turns that trepidation begins to seep in.

How am I ever going to find my way out of here?

Even if we're lucky enough to lose the Fetch, without my phone, a light, or any idea how to leave, I could die in these tunnels.

Before I could even finish the thought, I run back out into the middle of the circular room where we started.

Startled, I pull up short, shaking away the shock and confusion.

"Autumn—oh, thank god."

I spin around, clutching at my heart as Wade rushes toward me.

"How—? You shouldn't be in here. You could have been lost..." I sputter, trying to catch my breath. My body quakes from the rush of adrenaline, and I can't even begin to process what's happening.

Wade shakes his head. "It's a long story and I'll tell you everything. But first, I have the rest of the revenants... You haven't started the ritual yet, have you?"

"Noooo—" Cat's Fetch erupts from the catacombs tunnel behind me, rushing past me and racing at Wade like a wildfire. The air crackles behind her as if she's summoning some sort of static energy field.

As she reaches him, she places both hands across his chest, pushing hard. My mouth drops open as her body somehow passes through his, the way it had with Abigail. However, it doesn't exit the other side alone.

CHAPTER 26
ALL THINGS DISPLACED

W ade's spirit is thrust outside of his body, as if the Fetch was somehow able to dig inside him and yank it out. I nearly drop the grimoire as I lunge forward, reaching out for Wade. His physical body goes dormant—not unlike the revenant of his grandfather behind me. But his spirit stands just behind it, as if he's somehow managed to clone himself.

"Wade—" I call out, unable to make my brain come up with more words. My heart comes to a complete stop— refusing to beat, just in case this means what I fear it means. Instead, my brain scrambles, searching for any answers on how to put him back where he belongs.

The Fetch of Cat cackles, as if this is the most hilarious thing she's ever seen. "Looks like lover boy here isn't as invulnerable as he thinks he is."

Wade's spirit looks down at his ethereal body with wide eyes and a look of horror clear across his face. "How —?" he mutters, flitting his gaze between me and his body.

I shake my head, still unable to process.

What do I do? How do I make this right?

I'm in no way prepared for any of this... I barely managed to bring Cat to life, and I evidently screwed that up. How do I put Wade back into his body?

"Abigail—" I cry out, my voice cracking. She has to be able to help me...

The Fetch of Cat circles around Wade and his spirit, a look of determination painting her features.

Abigail flickers into the room, but only a glimmer of her former self. Whatever she did to try to stop the Fetch clearly drained her.

"Help me..." I say, pointing to Wade's body. "I don't know what to do."

Cat's Fetch steps forward, curiosity lighting up her eyes. She jabs a single pointer finger into Wade's spirit, but her hand goes right through him the way it did Abigail. Wade steps away, pulling back his arm and gawking at her. As if pleased with this outcome, she looks up, her eyes locking again on me.

Clutching the grimoire to my chest, I turn back to Abigail. Her essence shivers in and out of existence until she vanishes completely again.

Dammit.

Dropping to my knees, I flip through the pages of the grimoire, trying to find something—anything that makes sense. The words are a jumbled mess, and I don't even take in the pictures or symbols. It's like it's all Greek.

"There's no one here who can stop me now... Not you, not them," the Fetch says, walking around Wade's spirit.

Suddenly conscious of the predicament, Wade comes back to himself, and his spirit turns to face Cat's doppelgänger. "I wouldn't be so sure of that."

The Fetch shakes her head, completely unconcerned by his admonishment. Instead, the kinetic energy I felt as she ran by me rises again, making my hair stand on end. Behind me, the revenant gets restless as he begins to struggle against the energetic cord tying him to me.

"Tsk. What a predicament... Let's see, which one will you choose to fight first?" the Fetch says, smirking. "Do you save your lover boy here? Stop me from getting your grimoire? Or stop *him*?"

The revenant's extremities begin to twitch, its eyes widening with some kind of self-awareness he didn't have before. He grabs hold of the energetic cord, tugging on it hard. However, unlike a real rope, it doesn't pull me toward him, but it crackles under his cognizant touch. Instead, he turns his eyes to me, rushing forward and groping at the air. He stops just feet from my face, as if some sort of invisible fence separates the two of us.

While relief flashes through me, there's an undercurrent of crushing horror that threatens to engulf me. Without thinking, I close my eyes. I have to do the one thing I know how to do. I don't know how to stop a Fetch or inter a revenant, but I know how to save a soul.

Summoning as much energy as I possibly can, I draw on everything I've learned and lean on the power I have yet to understand. I may not have Abigail here to guide me —but I do have her gifts. My only hope is that it's enough... I don't have a sacred circle, candles...an offering. But one thing I know for sure is this is *not* his time. I can only hope the universe will side with me.

There's an enormous shift in the energy of the space as I tap into my innate gifts and birthright. This is my family's space—it's under our protection—and I'll be damned if

I let a Fetch or a friggin' zombie destroy hundreds of years of preservation. Determination settles over me and my eyes flick open.

Cat's doppelgänger steps back, concern flitting through her smug face for the first time.

Refusing to take my eyes off of her, I mutter under my breath, "Death—taker of life, power of gods and givers, grant me this request. Bone, blood, breath, flesh. Recover Wade's soul—his *remnants*—and return him to me."

"No—" the Fetch screams, her mouth open in horror as she rushes at me, stopping just inches from my face.

I hold my ground and continue to mutter the incantation. Wade's spirit encloses itself in a sort of cocoon, as it starts to slide toward his body like it's being pulled by a magnet.

Before his soul can merge with his body, Cat's Fetch charges, stepping into its place instead. As she vanishes, Wade's body animates again, despite his soul still being outside.

"Well, this is new..." Wade's hand rises as he looks at it with curiosity.

"Get out," I demand, taking a step forward. My pulse thrums like a hummingbird's wings as it hammers in my ears.

Without warning, Wade's body rushes at me and tackles me to the ground. The grimoire slides across the stone floor, landing a few feet away from the two of us.

"You know, it never occurred to me I couldn't actually interact with your book in my astral form," the Fetch says in Wade's voice as she claws her way up my body.

The strange cocoon around Wade's soul begins to dissipate and as he comes to himself, he rushes to my side.

Reaching down, he tries to lift his body from me, but his hands go straight though.

However, the weight of his physical body on top of me takes my breath away as Cat uses her newfound strength to pin me to the ground. Extending her reach, she tries to collect the grimoire, but the revenant's renewed fervor works against her as he kicks it out of the way.

Wade's body rolls off of mine and crawls its way to the book and I lurch forward, trying to pull him back. Instead, a sharp pain shoots through my torso and I curl over to catch my breath.

"Don't let me, er—" Wade's spirit calls out, racing forward again and trying to pull his body back, but unable to make contact with anything.

It doesn't seem the revenant is very discerning about who it attacks, as it reaches down, yanking Wade's body back by the hair. It's a byproduct I'm sure Cat's doppelgänger hadn't anticipated when she tried to wind it up like a toy soldier. She cries out, groping at the gnarly fingers.

A few feet away Abigail manages to materialize, her essence still not one hundred percent as she shimmers in and out of solidity. Her chin drops and she immediately turns her gaze to me.

"My apologies, Autumn. Please forgive me," she whispers.

Without warning, she enters my body, somehow managing to shove my consciousness aside. It's like being locked in a glass room—able to see everything that's going on but not able to interact with my surroundings.

Abigail uses me to push up to a kneel. With my pointer finger, she draws a symbol in the ground. It looks like three interconnecting triangles.

Though I want to fight back from the intrusion, despite myself, I can't help but wonder what she has planned next.

The Fetch shoves Wade's grandpa aside, crawling her way to the grimoire.

Abigail ignores it. Instead, she contorts my hands into various symbols, like some sort of magical sign language. Then, she uses my voice to say, "Hail all gods, goddesses, and protectors of the Temple of the Soul—each who weigh heaven and earth in delicate balance, and in honor of the Fates' grand plan. Oh mighty Death, taker of life, I deliver unto you the body of William Hoffman. Ashes to ashes, dust to dust, bless his body so it may slumber in eternal rest."

As her final words are spoken, the cord tying the revenant's body to mine disintegrates. When the last remnants of it fade from around his torso, every corner of his body turns to ash and blows away like glitter being blown into the breeze. It flits away, sparkling as it spirals into the depths of the tunnel behind us.

My body lurches forward as Abigail's energy is expelled, unable to hold onto my body. She's thrust outside, and once again, I'm in the driver's seat of my own body. Worse than before, her energy signature is weak, and her form is barely visible. Without a word, she vanishes completely.

Wade's body stands up, the grimoire clutched in his hands, as a monstrous smile bursts over his ordinarily handsome features. "Finally," the Fetch says, running a hand along the ancient cover.

"I—I don't know what to do? I don't know how to

help," Wade's spirit says, distressed. "Autumn, what do I do?"

Racing forward, I spring at the grimoire, determined to wrestle it away from the Fetch. She steps aside at the last moment and I narrowly miss. My shoulder hits the side of the catacombs wall and pain shoots down my arm.

"I could really get used to this," the Fetch says, chuckling, and running her hands up and down Wade's form. "I can see why you like this...creature. He *feels* good. Strong... There's a lot of power behind a male's body. Who knew?"

"Yeah, well, it's already spoken for—so get out," I say, twisting around and lunging for the book again.

This time, I make contact, grabbing hold of either side of the grimoire and tugging with all my might. Wade's strong hands hold steady, though, clutching at the grimoire as if my actions are nothing more than the feeble attempts of a toddler.

An ominous chuckle erupts from deep inside Wade's chest as the Fetch snatches the grimoire back. "You don't stand a chance. This was always my destiny. Don't you get that? You can take away the revenants, but I'll still find a way to become immortal."

"That's what you want? Immortality?" I sputter. "Why?"

Wade's silver eyes narrow. "See, this is why you shouldn't be in possession of this. How long have you known Cat was a Gemini Twin and you never even bothered to look it up... Typical."

"Then why don't you enlighten me," I fire back.

"Let's just say Colton shouldn't get all the fun." Pushing me aside, she tucks the grimoire under her arm and walks toward the tunnel exit. She doesn't even bother with me, as if she's realized just how irrelevant I am.

Feeling depleted and utterly defeated, desperation floods my system.

The walls are closing in and I can't breathe. If she walks out—how will I ever get Wade's soul back in his body? What if we can't? I realize now I'm fighting a battle I was sorely unprepared to fight.

One thing I know for sure—I can't let her take the book... and I can't let her take Wade's body...

But how can I possibly stop her?

CHAPTER 27
SUDDEN DEATH

Wade's soul reaches for me. "Autumn—did she hurt you? Are you okay?" His eyes are deep pools of concern as he places his ethereal hand against my cheek. The coolness of it seeps into my skin, making me shiver.

I shake my head. "No, I'm all right."

"Good," he exhales softly, lowering his eyebrows. "How do we stop her? There has to be a way..."

"I don't know..." I whisper, blinking back tears as I watch his body walk away without him.

Despair washes over me and tears brim in my lids.

Suddenly, dark clouds billow into the circular room, drawing all the energy from the torches and dimming the space. Wade's dad steps out of the black, billowy vortex, getting right between his son's hijacked body and the way out.

"Oh, shit," Wade's spirit curses.

His father doesn't say a word to the Fetch, but the

impact is immediate. Without a doubt, Cat's doppelgänger knows this means trouble.

Wade's body screeches to a halt, cowering and stumbling a few steps back with the book pulled in tightly. "No—no, no, no..."

As if somehow able to grow in size, Wade's dad towers over his son's body as he steps forward, extending a hand out in front of him, still in utter silence. His silver eyes flash and his nostrils flare as he waits for the Fetch to do as his suggestion requires.

Instead, the Fetch backs away, clutching the grimoire tighter. "No, no, I *need* it."

"Do not defy me, child," Wade's father says, his voice thundering through the space with an air of authority that makes my blood run cold.

"You don't understand, though."

Wade's dad rolls his eyes, and with the flick of his wrist, the book flies out of Wade's grip, landing softly in his father's arms. Wade's shoulders drop and the Fetch immediately drops to the floor, kneeling.

"I'm sorry, so, so sorry... Please," the Fetch murmurs, groveling at his feet.

I narrow my gaze, completely baffled.

What on earth is his dad?

What other powers could he possibly possess that would make the Fetch cower under his presence this way?

"Please—you have to understand. I only wanted what should be rightfully mine," Wade's voice quivers as the Fetch tries to reason.

Beside me, Wade's spirit shakes his head, covering his mouth with his hand. "That won't go down well."

"Of all the beings to displace, you chose very poorly,"

Wade's dad says, extending the arm with the grimoire in it. It floats from his hand, landing softly on the pedestal in the middle of the room. As it makes its way to its rightful place, the pedestal vanishes into the floor.

Whatever power it possesses is evidently not an allure for him.

The Fetch stands, looking longingly at it, but turns back to Wade's dad. "It wasn't about this body. I just—I needed to do something to stop the necromancer. Surely you can understand. She has the power to ruin everything. Please. Please just help me."

Wade's dad takes another ominous step forward. The room vibrates with immense power, radiating from him in waves. In an odd way, it's as if every molecule gravitates toward him, eliminating even the oxygen from the space, as it gets sucked into his energy.

"You are in no place to bargain, child. You shouldn't even be here," he says in a silky cadence.

The Fetch bows her head, agreeing. "You're right. Absolutely right. I should never have..."

"Just as with necromancers," Wade's dad flicks his gaze to me, "Gemini Twins are not to meddle with the natural laws of life and death. They are perfectly balanced as they are. Yet, there is always one of you who does not understand the beauty mortality possesses. *You* have already been gifted mercy in this duality, but you do not even see it for what it is. You yearn for something you can't possibly understand and demand to defy it. How incredibly petulant."

"Mercy? To grow old and die while your brother—your twin—can live forever? That's not mercy—" the Fetch begins, but stops short at the murderous look on the face of Wade's dad.

"Child, if anyone knows what mercy is in this regard, it's me. But if you believe you know better...perhaps we put it to the test. Perhaps immortality is just the punishment you deserve," he says, placing an enormous hand atop Wade's head.

Wade's body again drops to his knees as his Dad's entire appearance transforms before my eyes. Dark wings sprout from his back and his skin turns a dark shade of gray. His eyes glow like embers on a fire as he's suddenly clad in a pitch-black robe. If I didn't know better, I'd say he was a Dementor from Harry Potter—but they never had wings. Then, in his free hand, a scythe the color of blood materializes from the center of his palm outward. It glows brightly, emitting a repeating pulse of white and gold light.

Without a single word, Cat's Fetch is thrust from Wade's body. It lingers just outside, staring slack-jawed at the frame she just inhabited. Then, with a wave of his grey hand, the Fetch dismantles itself like burnt leaves floating on the wind. Pointing his scythe at the dancing orb of particles, Wade's dad redirects it all out the tunnel exit.

Horror and fascination threaten to consume me. Every cell in my body is suddenly alive with a deep, powerful knowing. I cover my mouth, squelching the need to cry out. Wade's father is no Dementor...

He's the Angel of Death.

Slowly, he turns his glowing amber gaze my way. Then, raising the hand from his son's body, he curls a finger in the air, summing me forward. I take a tentative step out of the shadows, my entire body jittery in the movement.

However, Wade's soul moves past me, cutting off my advance. Relief washes over me at first, but it's quickly replaced by dread.

"Wait," I cry out, coming to my senses. "Please, don't hurt him. None of this was his fault."

Wade's soul turns back to me, shooting me a lopsided grin. "I got this, Dru. And a little piece of advice... Don't ever bargain with him. It never ends well." Turning back to his father, Wade's soul moves forward until he comes to a stop just behind his lifeless, kneeling body.

"Do you see now?" the Angel of Death says, his voice a deeper, scarier version of itself. "The affairs of life and death are not to be trifled with."

Wade's soul nods. "I never doubted you on that."

"Then why?" his father asks, slowly transforming back into his human form.

I can barely imagine a place in this world where the Angel of Death even needs to ask a question like that.

"You already know why," Wade says softly, looking back at me.

Inhaling deeply, Wade's dad turns his gaze to the ceiling, as if asking for help from God. "There are millions of women—millions yet who have powers. Of all them who exist in this world, why would you choose to love...*a necromancer*? She defiles everything we stand for—everything we vow to protect and uphold. Is this a rebellion thing?"

Wade actually has the guts to snicker.

His father peers through his eyebrows. "You know the rules, Wade. One day soon you'll be taking your place by my side and you'll have to do what I do. You'll see all I see... I wish I could show you just how wrong it is. How wrong *her kind* is... Necromancy is a power that should never have existed."

"What's with all this *her kind, your kind* bullshit? She's a good person. Her heart is in the right place. She didn't ask for this gift—it's how she was born, for fucksake," Wade says, moving away from his body and his father. "You know what, if you're going to anoint me early, then just do it. But regardless of when, I'll still run things the way I see fit."

"You won't be allowed to stay with her," his father growls, stepping forward. "You will have duties to perform."

I swear, even the torches dim under the intensity of the anger bubbling to the surface.

Wade drops his chin to his chest and turns back around. "Isn't that what you want? For me to give up everything the way you did?"

Pinching the bridge of his nose, Wade's dad sighs heavily. "You know why I had to... If I could have stayed longer—"

"But you didn't, and you took Mom down with you," Wade spits. "And I've been here to pick up the mortal pieces alone. So forgive me if I don't give a damn about the legacy you want to impress upon me."

His father's face crumples, but his jaw sets. "I will not help you again. Death follows *this one* like the plague." He raises a finger to point at me and I jut out my chin. He ignores it and turns back to Wade. "Next time, no more games. No more defiance. You will take your place."

"Fine," Wade mutters under his breath.

"And I will not allow you use our assets to help—"

"I said *fine*," Wade repeats, practically spitting venom back at his dad.

"Wade—" I start, taking a cautious step forward. "Please be careful."

Wade shoots me a sideways glance and holds out a hand, telling me to stay back.

His father turns his penetrating gaze on me. Despite looking so much like the man I love, a terrifying shiver races up my spine and I clamp my mouth shut.

Sighing heavily, he extends a hand summoning Wade's soul. His spirit sweeps forward as if being sucked forward without his consent. Then, with the flick of his dad's wrist, Wade's soul is thrust back inside his body.

Instantly, Wade crumples over, sputtering for air and groping at his chest. Despite myself, I rush forward, reaching out and wrapping my arms around him.

"Final chance," his father whispers.

"I heard you," Wade says, taking deep breaths and pushing himself up to stand.

I stay beside him, offering my shoulder to lean against as I wrap my arm around his waist. His father peers down at me, as if still confused by what his son is doing with someone like me...and truth be told, a part of me is beginning to wonder the same thing.

After a moment under his scrutiny, his presence becomes overpowering, and I fight the odd urge to kneel at his feet.

"I am not the only one whose radar you've fallen upon. You have many choices ahead of you, Autumn Blackwood. I hope you choose them well," he says, peering down at me from the bridge of his nose.

"I'll do my best," I say, forcing my words to sound more confident than I actually feel.

I mean, Death doesn't want me around his son...and is telling me directly not to fuck up. That's kinda trippy.

"If it wasn't for the fact that your father helped me in the past, and your ancestors have taken up the task as keepers of these sacred catacombs—your lineage would have been extinguished centuries ago."

I blink wide-eyed back at him, unsure what to say to something like that.

Taking another step closer, he lowers his eyebrows and cocks his head. "So help me, if you put my son's soul in jeopardy again, I will not hesitate to extinguish your lineage anyway. No matter the bargains of your ancestors. Are we clear?"

Panic sweeps through me and I nod, unable to form words.

"Excellent," he says, straightening up and adjusting the end of his sleeve. "Now then, I believe this belongs to you." He holds his hand out, offering me something.

I extend a shaky palm, unsure I want to take anything from the Angel of Death. Particularly after he just threatened me.

When my hand is directly beneath his, he lets a single red thread fall. It's the size of a piece of yarn, but frayed and tattered like it's been chewed up and spat back out.

I look up, confused.

But he's gone.

CHAPTER 28
WHERE DO WE GO FROM HERE?

I barely remember the next blur of events, as Wade somehow manages to summon the rest of the revenants into the main chamber. By some strange miracle, they all file in, one after the other.

When the last of them shuffle in, fourteen in all, Wade turns expectantly. "You're up."

My mind churns through everything that's happened these past few hours and I nod absently.

Wade watches me with those deeply intense eyes of his and I stumble backward, realizing he means it's my job to inter them. Taking a deep breath, I call out, "Abigail, the rest of the revenants are here. We need your help."

Both of us stand shoulder to shoulder, scanning the rounded room, eyeing each of the tunnels in case she comes out of the darkness.

When nothing happens, Wade drops his chin, kicking softly at the dirt on the floor. The revenants don't seem to mind the delay; if anything, they seem perfectly content as they wait for their end.

Clearing my throat, I shrug and walk over to the spot in the middle of the room where the grimoire resides. I mull over how I intend to use it, considering how I can't even read any of the pages. As I get closer, the stone pedestal rises, almost as if it senses me.

When the pedestal reaches its full height, I pause, letting my fingertips trace the symbols on the cover. One of them stands out, now vaguely familiar after Abigail used me to draw it. The triple triangle, overlapping and inter-locking through itself.

Wade watches me from across the room, waiting patiently to see what I plan on doing. His expression is almost expectant, like he thinks I have it in me to do this without Abigail... But I know better.

Shaking my head, I flip open the grimoire, unsure if I should even be bothering with the book. The words Abigail spoke before have settled in the back of my mind and maybe, just maybe, I could conjure them up again without the book.

Yet, as I stare down at the pages, my mouth falls open. Everything—every word written—has somehow managed to rearrange itself into an intelligible order. I take it all in, unable to believe my eyes.

How is this possible? Is it the book? Or was it something else that's allowed this to happen?

"What is it? Is everything okay?" Wade says, taking a tentative step towards me.

"Yeah. It's just—" I tug my eyebrows in and nod. "Long story. But I think I can still do this."

Wade sighs in relief. "Good. I don't overly wanna babysit these guys for long."

I shoot him a grin of agreement and turn back to the

enormous tome. Flipping through the pages, I scan each one, looking for the right spells. When I find it, I bend in, studying the words, suddenly able to make sense of what Abigail was doing.

Lifting the grimoire off the pedestal, I walk around it to face the revenants. Then, dropping down, I balance the book on my left knee. Closing my eyes, I tune into the energies around me. The lifeless revenants and the beating heart of Wade. There's a special quality to each, and it sings me a lullaby that I hadn't heard before.

When I feel as though I've centered myself, I open my eyes. With my pointer finger, I draw the interconnected triangles into the dirt a few feet in front of the revenants.

As if from muscle memory, or perhaps whatever memories linger from Abigail, my hands easily form the symbols needed to inter the bodies and inanimate them. As I do so, each of their eyes glass over with a hazy blue film.

Glancing at Wade from the corner of my eye, his face is open in bewildered amazement.

I stand up, holding open the grimoire so it's right in front of me. I feel almost like a minister about to marry two people, not lay a horde of them to rest.

Clearing my throat, I stand tall. My words come out a bit scratchy at first, but grow in strength. "Hail all gods, goddesses, and protectors of the Temple of the Soul—each who weigh heaven and earth in delicate balance, and in honor of the Fates' grand plan. Oh mighty Death, taker of life, I deliver unto you the bodies before me. Ashes to ashes, dust to dust, bless them all, so they may slumber in eternal rest."

As I speak the words, I realize it was likely these very

words that called Wade's father to us. The power in them is not innate from me or even my family—but rather, from death itself.

Seconds after the final word is spoken, each of the bodies standing before me fades away, just as Wade's grandfather had. Their solid bodies disintegrate into small, glittery granules as they're extracted from this chamber and entombed in their final resting place. Each body escapes through one of the ten remaining tunnels as if the catacombs themselves know exactly where they should be settled.

When all of them are gone, and Wade and I are alone, I close the grimoire. Exhaling in relief, I stare at the empty space in front of me.

It's done...

Beside me, Wade also breathes out, but as he turns to face me, his expression is clouded with worry. I pull the book in tight, using it almost as a protective shield.

There's so much we need to discuss now. So much that needs to be laid out straight. But I don't know if I'm ready for any of it yet.

He takes three giant strides over to me, wrapping his arms around my shoulders and pulling me in tight. "Autumn, I—"

Before I can stop them, tears stream down my cheeks as the torrent of emotions I've been bottling up release. I lean into him but shift to gently place the grimoire at my feet.

"Wade, I know there's so much..." I begin.

This time, he places both hands along the sides of my face. His lips bear down on mine, and the room swirls with a heady need for him. Reaching up, I entwine my fingertips into his hair, and pull him closer.

Whatever we are... Whatever this is... I don't even care. All I know is we have each other right here, right now. Wade's alive and his soul is back where it ought to be.

When he finally pulls back, breaking our kiss, he places his forehead against mine. "Autumn, I'm sorry about everything. About Colton— I know you weren't keeping things from me to hurt me. It's just I..."

"I know," I say, shaking my head. Lifting my gaze to his, I fixate on his beautiful eyes—those extraordinary silver eyes.

His pupils widen, but the more I stare into their depth, the more I'm overcome by their magic. They say the eyes are the windows to the soul, and after witnessing his firsthand, I can without a doubt say it's absolutely true. Everything about him, his whole essence, it's all right there in those tiny, magnificent orbs.

"I should have told you, and you have no idea how many times I wanted to. Or I thought I should. I just..." I sigh, trying to find the right words. "I just want you to be happy and I couldn't bear the thought of hurting you. Even if I wanted nothing to do with it."

"None of it matters," he says, running his thumb across my eyebrow. "Being thrust into the aether has a way of putting everything into perspective."

"But what about..." I bite my lip, unable to finish the sentence. It's not a path I'm overly ready to go down, but one I need to, nonetheless.

"I know you have so many questions and I promise to answer them all. I wish I could have answered them for you earlier, I truly do," Wade says, his eyebrows crumpling in the middle.

"Why couldn't you?" I ask, dropping my arms and sliding my hands inside his.

He inhales sharply through his nose and tilts his head. "Our kind is sworn to secrecy. If the wrong people were to find the lineage for the Angel of Death...well, let's just say there could be consequences if that information got into the wrong hands."

"So, it's true then," I whisper, dropping my gaze. "You're an Angel of Death?"

I look up to meet his burdened eyes. "Not yet. Not until I die."

His words hit me like a punch in the gut. That's why he had said what he did about anointing him early. Had his father wanted to, he could have claimed his soul right then and there.

My words come out in a hushed sob. "But your dad— he let you stay..."

Wade lifts his left hand, brushing aside a strand of my hair and tucks it behind my ear. "He did."

I swallow hard. "But he doesn't want you to be with me. He doesn't think—"

"I don't give a damn what he thinks," Wade says, pressing his lips into a thin line.

"But you should," I cry. "My god, Wade. Death. He's...*Death*."

Wade chuckles as he nods. "He is. So is my grandpa now. And my great-great grandpa...and so on and so forth. There will be plenty of time for death and he knows that."

I shake my head. "I don't understand."

"We get one lifetime. One experience here on this

mortal realm. With the exception of my father's misguided rule about necromancers, he doesn't have a say in how I live it," Wade says, smiling. "And as you can see, even there, he doesn't have much say."

"But——?" I begin, trying to process all of this.

"Look," Wade says, squeezing both of my hands. "The way I see it, we're perfect for each other. I have no powers at all until I ascend. I get flashes, maybe a few insights... strange sensations and vibes. That's all. But in the meantime, I study. And I can live vicariously through you. Besides, I still say our meeting in the cemetery was fate at play, Dru."

His nickname for me resonates like a jolt to the heart and my mouth pops open.

"Angel..." I whisper, taking a step back and brushing my mouth with my fingertips. "I nicknamed you Angel."

Wade snickers softly, as he grins and drops his chin. "Yeah, I was ridiculously pleased about that. Believe me, there's been more than a couple of times I've chuckled to myself about it. See? *Fate*..."

I drop his hand, suddenly unable to take in much more. I pick up the grimoire, walking it back to its pedestal as I process. As I place it back on top, the pedestal descends back into the floor. I stand there, staring at it as it vanishes from view.

There are so many questions knotting themselves together and I'm not sure how to sort them all out. If he's next in line to become an Angel of Death—how do we make sure he has a good, long life?

Like the billowing black clouds his dad appears from, fear begins to take over.

What if his dad is right... what if death does follow after me?

I lift my gaze to him, trying to squelch the panic rising from the center of my torso.

What if his dad's rule has nothing to do with necromancy or me? What if his rule is to protect Wade so he lives that good, long life?

What if being with me is actually putting his life at risk?

To my right, Abigail's form flickers in and out of reality, making me jump. Her face is contorted in an odd expression of fear and horror as she tries to speak to me. Her arms splay out wide, and at first her words don't reach me, despite her clearly trying to communicate.

Confused, I shake my head. "What is it? I can't understand you... What are you trying to say?"

Abigail reaches out to me, then vanishes again, only to pop up on my left side.

"What's going on?" Wade asks, his eyes floating around the space.

Abigail bends forward, her face inches from my neck. A frigid cold creeps up my neck as she whispers into my ear, "You need to be ready. His time has come."

To Be Continued in Book 3: Haunted Legacy.
Start Reading Now!

NEXT IN THE WINDHAVEN
WITCHES SERIES...

What did Abigail mean when she said, 'His time has come'? Is Wade's time coming to an end? Or did she mean someone else?

Find out by reading **Haunted Legacy**, *Book 3 of the Windhaven Witches*!

START READING NOW!

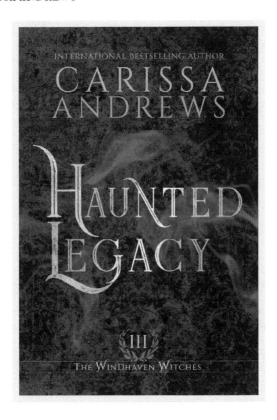

Being haunted by ghosts isn't unusual for Autumn, but this time it's someone she didn't think was dead.

A utumn's world is a life of ghosts, death, and destruction. The last thing she wants is to be the cause of her boyfriend's early demise. Especially when she's already been warned by the Angel of Death to stay away from him. So, to keep Wade safe, there's only one thing to do: end it.

But of course, fate doesn't let them off the hook that easy. Thrust together for a school project, Wade is put right in the line of fire when an unexplained, and surprisingly violent, haunting erupts at Blackwood Manor.

To figure out how to stop it, Autumn has to communicate with the spirit, but it will do anything to protect its identity. The deeper Autumn digs, the more sinister the truth becomes. Devastated and vulnerable, Autumn has to face the facts and find a way to end the ghost's deadly attacks. Otherwise, both she and Wade will become the ghost's next victim.

THE WINDHAVEN WITCHES

Secret Legacy *(Sept 15, 2020)*
Soul Legacy *(Oct 6, 2020)*
Haunted Legacy *(Nov 3, 2020)*
Cursed Legacy *(Dec 1, 2020)*

ALSO BY CARISSA ANDREWS

THE PENDOMUS CHRONICLES

Trajectory: *A Pendomus Chronicles Prequel*

Pendomus: *Book 1 of the Pendomus Chronicles*

Polarities: *Book 2 of the Pendomus Chronicles*

Revolutions: *Book 3 of the Pendomus Chronicles*

DIANA HAWTHORNE SUPERNATURAL
MYSTERIES

Oracle: *Book 1*

Amends: *Book 2 (February 26, 2021)*

Immortals: *Book 3*

Vestige: *Book 4*

Harbinger: *Book 5*

Pantheon: *Book 6*

THE 8TH DIMENSION NOVELS

The Final Five: *An **Oracle** & **Awakening** Bridge Novelette*

Awakening: *Rise as the Fall Unfolds*

Love is a Merciless God

ABOUT THE AUTHOR

Carissa Andrews
Sci-fi/Fantasy is my pen of choice.

 Carissa Andrews is an international bestselling indie author from central Minnesota who writes a combination of science fiction, fantasy, and dystopia. Her plans for 2020 include publication of her highly anticipated ***Windhaven Witches*** series. As a publishing powerhouse, she keeps sane by chilling with her husband, five kids, and their two insane husky puppies, Aztec and Pharaoh.

To find out what Carissa's up to, head over to her website and sign up for her newsletter:
www.carissaandrews.com

facebook.com/authorcarissaandrews

twitter.com/CarissaAndrews

instagram.com/carissa_andrews_mn

amazon.com/author/carissaandrews

bookbub.com/authors/carissa-andrews

goodreads.com/Carissa_Andrews

Printed in Great Britain
by Amazon

76648485R00158